# STRIPPED BARE

REBECCA CASTLE

ISBN: 9780645395945

# PROLOGUE

The first thing that hits you on stage is the screaming.

It's like a wall of noise launching from across the room with enough force to bowl you over. It doesn't even matter if you're standing behind the curtain like I am; you're going to be hit with the screaming no matter what. And it's gonna be hard, trust me.

*Here we go.*

For the first brief second once you step up onto the stage, your senses are completely obliterated by the noise. Don't worry, it's normal. Give it another second. Your ears will get used to it.

I've done this hundreds of times, and it still takes me a moment to get used to the sound of a hundred screaming women.

*Get ready.*

Once your ears are adjusted to the noise, then you pick up on the music hidden below the screaming. A thudding rhythm that rocks your body to the core. You can feel it pumping its way through your veins. It's the music that unlocks the adrenaline in you, the music that makes excitement course freely through your body.

*Can you feel it? The tingle?*

As a red-blooded male, there's no choice but for your deep-seated primal man's instinct to burst out of its cage as you gear up ready to dance. It makes you feel fearless. It makes you feel goddamn sexy. How can it not when there's a room full of women noisily anticipating your naked body?

Fight or flight?

*Oh, I'm here to fight.*

It's pretty overpowering, the life of a male stripper.

And I can't get enough of it. I'm *addicted*.

The sweat.

The body oil.

The heat.

The excitement.

The adrenaline.

The cheering of the female audience as a hundred ovaries scream at you to just *fuck* them. Urgently. Right here. Right now.

How can I not feel like a man when it's like this? That I'm not on top of the world? How can I not feel like the sexiest man in the universe when I have a roomful of women at my feet?

You can't blame me if I do.

If there's one thing I've learned from doing this for a living, it's that women want an alpha man. They absolutely *crave* a strong guy to step in and take control of their desires.

Not a boy.

A *man*.

Hey, hey, hey, not to say that women aren't strong or independent in their own right - I *really* don't want to sound like I'm another dumb misogynistic man - but there's something ferociously naturalistic for women to desire a man who they know will, and trust to, take control in the bedroom.

They want a man who can turn them on. A man who can make them *feel* something. A man brave enough, and strong enough, to dare take control of their pleasure. Women want to submit themselves to a true alpha man.

What I'm basically saying here is that women need their fantasies to feel sexy.

And I'm the one man in a million able to provide it.

Even the women who lead armies - even the ones who lead *countries* - sometimes just simply want to let down their hair and get rough and dirty.

Sometimes every woman just wants to let their inner sex goddess free.

And I'm the guy they turn to in their times of need. The dangerous loner who knows how to move his body. The man with the killer abs and the smoldering look who can promise you a good time and really, truly mean it.

I'm that guy.

And women want me because they know - they *instinctively* know - that I am good at sex.

And I'll let you in on a little secret.

I am fucking *awesome* at sex.

Oh, I know what you're thinking. *Here he is, another chauvinistic male thinking he's a big deal.*

But I can assure you it isn't bragging. I'm not being arrogant.

What I'm saying is a *fact*.

I'm simply good - simply *amazing* - at sex. Believe me, I've had plenty of goes at it. Look, being a male stripper means you get to see more pussy than any other man. Well, besides from a gynecologist.

And that's not even a problem. With the amount of

pussy I've seen, I'm practically a qualified vagina doctor by now, anyway.

Trust me when I say that women want me.

And I want them.

For all those women sitting out there in the club tonight sipping their Prosecco and cocktails, I am exactly what they're looking for. I am their escape from their boring lives and even more boring husbands, even if it's just for one night and even if I never touch them. I am the man they fantasize about. I bet I can do things to their body with just one smoldering look from the stage that no man has ever been able to accomplish in the bedroom. I symbolize their *freedom*.

I'm sorry to say, guys, but I'm the dude your woman dreams about when her head touches the pillow at night after a lousy sex session with you. I'm the guy that makes your girl bite hard on her pen in the middle of the workday when she starts to drift off, daydreaming about that one time they went to a male strip club and saw that incredible stripper. I'm the dude your girl is thinking of when she's all alone and she's touching herself in places on her body you never have the *balls* to go to.

That's my service. I provide that dream.

I'm the alpha man.

And pleasuring women is my *honor*.

And that's why I get to stand here, behind a thin curtain on the stage of a strip club, as a hundred drunk women scream my name in unison with the announcer.

I stand, ready for my big entrance, because I know they want me. Thousands of years of female evolutionary desire have led to me standing here tonight.

My muscles are tense. My cock is hard.

I'm already not wearing much, and soon I will practically be wearing nothing.

And, as I stand there, I can hear the announcer through the curtain. He's barely audible above the female screams, even with a microphone.

"Are you lovely ladies ready for the main event?"

*Yes!*

"The one you sexy women are all here tonight for?"

*Yes!*

"The one that knows exactly what to do to get you all hot and bothered?"

*Yes!*

"He's going to give you his marching orders. Wait until you see his weapon."

*Yes!*

"If you want him, he's locked and loaded."

*YES!*

"You know who he is. Give it up for the one and only... *CAPTAIN CHASE.*"

The curtain falls away.

The lights turn to me.

The music gets louder. The screaming intensifies.

And I start to strip.

# 1

*ANNA*

THE LAST PLACE on a Sunday night I will never, ever want to be at is Club Xstasy, and the very last seat in said club I would ever want to be seated in is the front row.

But I'm here. At Club Xstasy. At an actual male strip club. In the freaking front row.

I don't believe it.

Me.

Anna Jensen.

The girl whose high school nickname was *Little Miss Stuck-Up* is at a strip club on a Sunday night.

The girl who can't even bear any public displays of affection. Who winces at a couple kissing in a restaurant.

Me. At a place actually called *Xstasy*. And yep, it's spelled just like that. Someone - presumably someone incredibly drunk - actually signed off on that name.

In case you can't tell already, this is not my natural habitat. No, sir. This truly is the very *last* place I would ever want to be.

But I'm here.

I fold my arms and sink into my premium front row seat. The stage is level right at my breasts.

*Perfect.*

I can see everything. I've already decided that if I'm going to be forced to be here, then I'm going to remain as still as possible throughout the entire show. I don't want to attract any attention, and I've actually been pretty successful so far. No abs, or – even worse – *dicks* have been thrust in my face just yet. I've just got to remain completely still and I won't be made a target.

I sigh.

*Why, oh why, am I not at home?*

Someone jabs me in the ribs. I flinch, surprised. I'm pleased to discover it isn't a stripper's dick.

Instead, it's Erin, my best friend and work colleague. She flashes her big smile at me and lifts a glass of bubbling gold liquid towards my face. She's either oblivious to my exasperation at being here, or she's deliberately ignoring it.

"Here," she says, offering the glass. "Have some champagne, Anna."

It's the break between dancers. And even though nothing is happening on stage, it hasn't dampened the enthusiasm of the crowd, which seems to be one hundred percent female.

*What is it about a room of scantily clad muscular bimbo men that makes previously strong and previously independent businesswomen lose their freaking minds?*

Well, it's certainly not for me, that's for sure.

"You know I don't really drink," I reply to my friend, struggling to be heard over the screaming of a hundred women around me.

"Take it," Erin says, giving me a quick evil eye. "Come

on, it's Daria's bachelorette party. You don't want to upset the bride-to-be, do you?"

I stare back at her, uncompromising.

"I'm not getting drunk, especially not in here, Erin."

My best friend pleads at me through her big brown Bambi-like eyes. *"Come on,* Anna. It's a night out. Let your hair down."

I am unmoved.

"Nope."

She waves the champagne glass even closer towards me. "Please, Anna. You can stop being so prim and proper and *hoity-toity* for one single night. You need to loosen up. You need to relax. Do it for Daria."

*Alright, then.*

"Don't be such a downer, Anna."

"I'm not a downer," I snap back before taking the glass off her and angrily sipping on it. Erin smiles again.

"I knew you'd come round to it."

"One drink. That's it."

"Good, that's the spirit," Erin laughs.

I shake my head at my best friend, and I glance over to Daria over her shoulder. The bride-to-be is sitting a few more seats down from Erin and me in the exact middle of the front row. When we got to the club and I realized how close we were to the stage, I made sure I sat as far to the side as possible in my attempt to hide away from any kind of stripper-audience interaction, which means that I'm quite far from Daria and the rest of the bachelorette party.

And now it's time for the next act.

Erin's screaming equally loud as everyone else in the room. Practically *begging* for the next stripper.

Great.

Truth be told, I'm not even good friends with Daria. Sure, I've been invited to her wedding and to her bachelorette party, but it was more to do with me being best friends with Erin and also because we all work together in the same company, even though Daria's a receptionist on a level below mine. Unlike me, my best friend is the outgoing type. Erin's friends with everyone at work, so just being in association with her means I got an invite to this party.

And I didn't want to go until Erin forced me into it.

*It'll be fun.*

That's what she said.

And I, without thinking it through, relented.

I should've known how bad it'll be. Now I regret ever saying yes.

But I think the main reason I've been invited to the bachelorette party of some random colleague I barely even know is all to do with the sole fact my family's name hangs above the thirty-story skyscraper where we all work.

Dad's the boss of the company. You can't *not* invite his only daughter when you want to move up the greasy corporate pole.

It doesn't even matter why I'm here; the problem is that now I'm sitting on the front row of Xstasy, and the announcer has walked back on stage.

*Oh, brother. We're back to it.*

How long is this show going to go on for?

The announcer winks at the audience. He's half-naked himself. Just a few leather belts seem to be the only things preventing him from fully exposing himself to us. The female screams reach a hundred decibels as he raises his microphone to his lips.

I wonder if you could legally charge any of the dancers here with indecent exposure. Meh. It probably won't hold up in court when the judge rules that everyone here except for me seems to be begging for it.

*Are you lovely ladies ready for the main event?*

The lights go down.

*The one you sexy women are all here tonight for?*

The music gets louder.

*The one that knows exactly what to do to get you all hot and bothered?*

I sink even further into my seat. I grip my champagne glass so tightly I'm worried it may crack.

*He's going to give you his marching orders. Wait until you see his weapon.*

Next to me, Erin starts to scream uncontrollably. A ball of spit from her mouth even reaches the stage. I realize I must be the most sober woman in the club. By a lot.

*If you want him, he's locked and loaded.*

I roll my eyes.

*You know who he is. Give it up for the one and only...* CAPTAIN CHASE.

The red curtain behind the announcer falls away to reveal Club Xstasy's top attraction.

And, despite my eye rolls, even I can understand why he's their main event.

Captain Chase is *the* perfect male stripper. At the very least six feet tall, with probably one hundred and eight pounds of pure muscle, the man is a walking, breathing Adonis. A prize male specimen right in front of us lucky ladies. Top condition. He's wearing a dark green army vest which reveals his thick broad shoulders and some incredibly short - *and even tighter* - khaki shorts. Black leather boots strapped to his feet. And an army cap fitted just above the dark Aviator sunglasses.

And a perfect white grin.

Yeah, I get it.

*Captain* Chase.

He's an Army stripper.

*Ha ha, very funny.*

It's cheesy, but even I have to admit I feel something in my ovaries when he appears.

And so too does every other woman in Club Xstasy as well, it seems. I can't blame them. It's simply an evolutionary... *appreciation* for a well-built man, alright?

The music gets even louder, and Captain Chase – who I can safely presume is not a real soldier in the United States Army – begins to dance.

He lowers his Aviators so that we can all glimpse his deep green eyes. I glance around me at his enraptured audience. The gorgeous stripper's glare is like a laser, inducing an involuntary spasm in the nether regions of every girl he stares at. Luckily, I'm spared from his weapon. I must be immune.

He thrusts out his groin to the rhythm of the beat, the outline of his very large cock pretty visible underneath his tight army shorts. There's not much left to the imagination.

He flashes another wicked grin.

*Oh, he's clearly enjoying this.*

His cock is rock hard, I see.

The women around me scream in unbridled glee as he continues to dance. It's amazing to watch how much he controls the room.

He moves his hips in the same way I expect he does when he's bringing a partner to the brink of orgasm. He's a real pro, I'll give him that.

Still dancing, he makes his way down the stage. Towards the front row and, I quickly realize, towards me.

His muscles ripple with every move. His biceps must be the size of my head. His pecs practically scream to be let free from the vest caging them in.

I slide further back in my seat as he approaches the front row, gripping my glass even tighter. I really am refusing to be turned on by this guy. Yeah, sure, he's hot.

Totally in a purely primal sense. But I don't fall for guys who might have the body to die for but probably have nothing going on upstairs between their perfectly shaped ears.

Unlike Erin, I'm not the type of girl to scream for some muscular hunk to impregnate me, no matter how good his dancing skills are. No matter how orgasm-inducing his smile is.

I stay completely still in my seat, refusing to participate in the audience's screaming as so-called Captain Chase slides on over to the front of the stage. He gets down on his knees in front of our bachelorette party. Inches away from me and my tense, anxious body.

*Right.*

He's going to start thrusting his member in our faces. I get it. It's a routine. And we're all meant to go wild. Yadda, yadda.

My eyes dart towards the exit.

*Can I somehow get out of here without anyone noticing?*

This is definitely not what I want to be doing on a Sunday night.

But then I realize looking for the exit's a mistake.

Because Captain Chase has noticed it.

I glimpse the recognition in his eyes as he looks at me. He knows *exactly* what I'm thinking.

And he smirks at me. I'm so close to him I can see his dimples.

*Oh, God. He knows.*

Suddenly his big hand is reaching out towards me, beckoning me to join him on stage.

*Oh no. Oh no. Oh no.*

Not this. Anything but this.

I wave over towards Daria. "She's the bride," I shout to the dancer. "She should get a dance."

It doesn't work. He ignores my protestations. He moves his hand closer to mine.

*Yeah, he's doing this deliberately because he knows I'm the one woman in the club who doesn't want to be here.*

Even Daria doesn't care. It seems like she'll prefer me to have the private dance over her.

Great.

Erin is screaming next to me. I feel her grab at my wrist, pushing me towards the stage. She takes the champagne glass from me.

I am being *forced* on stage. Against my will.

And no one is going to help me.

In fact, it seems like everyone is working against me. The rest of the bachelorette party is yelling at me to get up there. It seems like the whole world wants me in the arms of Captain Chase.

Like a puppeteer, Erin brings my hand up to Captain Chase's and, before I know it, he's lifting me up.

"No, no, no," I struggle. It doesn't work. At all.

I'm already on the stage.

Captain Chase's grip is strong and unflinching. He guides me across the stage effortlessly. It's like he's levitating me. Suddenly I'm gently pushed into a chair that's seemed to appear behind me out of nowhere.

I blink and turn my head towards the audience. The stage lights are blinding, but I can just make out Erin and the rest of the bachelorette party in the front row. They're laughing and whooping at this crazy sight. Daria is leaning back in her seat in tears of laughter, her drink spilling everywhere.

I bet it must be hilarious to them. Me. The most *uptight* girl they know, about to receive a lap dance in front of a hundred women in a male strip club.

*Oh, yeah, it's such fun. Not.*

I can't escape. I can't get out of here. I'm stuck in a chair on stage, being laughed at by a room full of drunk women.

And then the music shifts into a military-style parade drill.

And Captain Chase and his dance moves become the only things I can see.

"Please," I whimper. He either ignores me or he can't even hear me above the military music.

He presses himself against me, his body grinding against my crotch in beat with the music. My mouth hangs open.

He leans over so that his full lips are against my ear. "This is all for you, sweetheart," he whispers. "Enjoy every moment of it."

"You're only doing this because you know I don't want to be here," I reply in a flat tone.

"You will be after I'm done with you."

"Nope. It isn't happening. You really should just take me back to my seat and have your way with the bride-to-be."

All Captain Chase does in response is to smile at me.

And it's infuriating.

But also kinda hot.

*Ugh.*

He moves against me like he's fucking me nice and slow. It's very hard to resist being turned on by this, but I try. Unsuccessfully.

And then he pulls back.

And he starts to strip.

*Oh, God.*

He rips off his vest. The crowd goes wild. And even I do, inside.

His torso is even more muscular than I expected. He's oiled up. A nicely shaped six-pack. Pecs I just want to run my hands over.

*Ugh.*

So incredibly, annoyingly good-looking.

To the sheer delight of the audience, he unbuckles his belt, letting his tight Army shorts fall to the ground.

He's wearing a thong. One with the Star-Spangled Banner imprinted on it.

I seriously doubt the American flag on a piece of sexy underwear was exactly what the Founding Fathers had in mind when they signed the Declaration of Independence.

But, like the rest of him, it's still pretty damn *hot*.

I know, I know. I've gone crazy for this handsome hunk stripping in front of me, just like all the women at Club Xstasy. I'm really no different from the rest of them. I guess it was only a matter of time before I became a fully signed-up member of the Captain Chase female fan club.

And now, naked except for his underwear, I can really see the outline of his cock. And it is *huge*.

I bet he drowns in pussy every night.

Captain Chase doesn't miss a beat. He sidles back up to me and runs his hands down my arms. He leans in close. His lips brush against my cheek. And he continues to gyrate right up against me.

And I nearly pass out.

"Captain Chase, everyone!" The announcer is back. "Stand at ease, soldier."

Suddenly my little not-so-private dance is over, and Captain Chase pulls back from me. He takes my hand and guides me to the front of the stage as the announcer continues to hype up the group dance coming up next.

Captain Chase lifts me back down to my seat. I turn around to thank him, but he's already gone.

I fall into my chair, completely exhausted. The rest of the bachelorette party is gathered around me, squealing in ecstasy at what just happened. I just fan myself and try to collect my thoughts.

That was an out-of-body experience.

*Wow.*

I lost my cool there for a second. For a moment on stage, I really had turned into another one of the screaming women in the crowd.

*Did I... actually enjoy myself up there?*

Surely not.

I turn to Erin. "I think I'll have another drink," I say.

I need it.

# 2

*ANNA*

I REALLY, really need to go for a pee.

I lean over to Erin. "I need to go."

"What?"

She can't hear me over the music. The group dance on stage is reaching the climax of their routine. *Pony* by Ginuwine is blasting out from the loudspeakers.

Yeah. All very *Magic Mike*. How cliché.

"I need to go to the bathroom," I yell into my best friend's ear. Now she can hear. She nods at me and I squeeze out of my seat and stumble over her on the way out of our row.

I've clearly drunk too much champagne.

*Please don't fall over and make an ass of yourself.*

I stagger around the seats and all the squealing women towards the bar area. I can't even see properly. Everything's hazy. Probably the result of drinking, like, six glasses of champagne in one go.

*Oh, God.*

Look, I'm not usually like this. Not at all. I'm not a big drinker, but after that *very* public lap dance Captain Chase performed for me on stage only like twenty minutes ago, I really needed a drink. Or six. I gulped down that bubbly golden liquid like there's no tomorrow.

And now I really need to pee.

And worse than that, I'm clearly *very* drunk.

*Well, that was quick to happen.*

I'm such a lightweight.

I make my way to the back of the club, my legs unsteady. I have to grip on the back of chairs to maintain balance. I very nearly trip over a stray high-heeled-foot.

Oops.

*Anna Jensen, get a hold of yourself.*

I see a door by the side of the bar. There's a little light above it. In my inebriated state, I can't clearly read the sign on the door, but I assume it's for the toilets. I stumble towards it and enter what seems to be a very long and very dark corridor.

*They don't make it easy to pee here, do they?*

I get to the end of the corridor. Turn the corner. Keep going.

I giggle at myself.

*Yep. So very drunk.*

You know what, though? Surprisingly, I think I've had a really good time tonight. That performance by Captain Chase, even though it was painfully embarrassing, was actually kinda fun. Something instinctual inside me responded to it.

Or maybe it's just the champagne bubbles.

The corridor leads into a hallway full of doors.

*What the...*

This is too difficult to navigate, especially when your

head is spinning out of control like mine is. I do a little dance on the spot. I really, really need to pee. Right now.

*Screw it.*

Trying my luck, I open the first door and step in.

"Oh, this isn't the bathroom," I slur to myself. It definitely isn't. There are bright lights. A full-length body mirror. Costumes. Hangers.

It's a dressing room.

*Oh, right. I've somehow made it backstage.*

I'm in a dancer's dressing room. No freaking way.

*Time to get out of here.*

But then I see it. On the other side of the room: an open door.

An open door leading into what obviously is a toilet.

I glance around.

*Well, I really need to pee and it's right there.*

And there's no one around. No one can catch me. It's either do pee there or do it here in my dress, and I'm not going to ruin what I'm wearing.

I sprint over to the toilet and duck inside. Just in time for me to manage to sit down on the toilet and let loose.

And the feeling is glorious.

*Yep, I really, really needed to do that.*

I'm in darkness. I didn't have time to turn on the light when I rushed in.

After I've peed, I stand at the basin and wash my hands. I look at myself in the mirror. Everything swirls around in my boozy vision.

I run my hands through my dark blonde hair. It's straight and long. My gray eyes stare back at me. I've never really had any major issues with my appearance, but looking at myself drunk makes me see everything with brand new eyes. I'm not *unattractive*, but I'm not the first girl guys go after. I've always been okay with that, though. I'm happy being independent. I'm happy being alone.

*Ugh, what am I even thinking? Stop indulging yourself, Anna Jensen, and get back to the bachelorette party.*

I turn to leave the toilet when someone steps in.

*Shit. I forgot to lock the door.*

The person flicks on the bathroom light, catching me red-handed, standing right in the middle of the room swaying on my feet.

*Oh shit, oh shit, oh shit.*

I know I shouldn't even be in here. I've screwed up big time.

It takes me a moment to register the person who's just walked in, but when I do, I freak out even more.

It's Captain Chase.

The stripper is standing in the doorway, staring at me. His expression is stoic.

"What are you doing in here?" he asks.

I open my mouth to reply, but then my eyes travel down his body.

And, with a gasp, I realize he's naked.

Completely and utterly naked.

"What are you doing in here?" Captain Chase repeats.

I'm not even properly listening to him. I'm just standing here, shocked at the... *massive* sight in front of me. I can barely squeak out the words. "Why are you naked?"

"This is my changing room," he replies slowly. "I'm getting changed. Why are you in here?"

I can't stop staring at his naked body.

At the absolute *monster* of a cock that hangs between his legs.

I gulp.

"I was... uh, looking for a bathroom. I needed to pee."

Captain Chase seems completely unbothered by the fact he's fully exposed in front of me. I guess he's been naked in front of a lot of women in his time. He's totally confident.

And it's kinda turning my drunk-ass self on.

"Hang on," he says, his green eyes narrowing. "I recognize you. Aren't you that chick in the front row?"

I snort. "The one you forcibly pulled onto stage?"

"The same one."

"Yep, that's me. Bingo. Ten points to Captain Chase."

"Thank you."

"It wasn't a compliment. I was being sarcastic."

The stripper chuckles. He finds me humorous.

*How dare he.*

"You seemed to enjoy my little show."

I shrug. God, the champagne's really getting to my head. "I did not."

Captain Chase's eyes seem to sparkle under the bathroom lights as he smirks at me. "Oh, I've been doing this a long time, Miss. I know when a woman's enjoying it."

"Really? Do you now?"

"Yes, I believe I do."

"Well, I wasn't."

"I bet you were. I saw that look of lust in your eyes. You're no different from any other woman who's been on the receiving end of my routine."

"You're so cocky," I reply, trying my best to stand up straight.

He winks. "That's a fun word."

I wave a hand at the exposed space between his legs.

"I didn't think of the word because of your dick, if that's what you're implying."

*Are we... flirting?*

If I wasn't so drunk, I'll be freaking out that I'm talking to a strange naked man in his dressing room, but the champagne has overridden my fears. It's turned me - *god forbid* - horny.

Captain Chase is right. I did enjoy his dance. And I'm currently enjoying the sight of his veiny dick a few inches away from my vagina.

"I have every right to be cocky," he replies.

"And what are you going to do with a strange woman in your dressing room?" I ask. "Especially when you're so... *naked.*"

The words just fall out of my drunk mouth.

But I'm not regretting them.

This is fun.

"I don't think we're *strangers*, are we? I mean, I think we were pretty well acquainted out there on the stage, don't you think?"

"You're right there," I reply. "But you don't even know my name."

I take a step towards the muscular man. He doesn't flinch. He doesn't back away. He is completely comfortable being so goddamn naked in front of me. Well, there's nothing that he should be ashamed of with a cock that large.

"What should I call you then, Miss?" he asks. His mouth has turned into a very wide grin. He's luring me in like a moth to a flame and I'm utterly unable to resist.

"Anna."

*Oh, I want this. I want what's coming.*

We both know what's about to happen.

"Cute name."

I giggle and slowly reach out with my hand, touching one of his oiled-up pecs with the tip of my finger. The stripper doesn't move. He lets me play with his ripped torso. "And why, pray tell, are you called *Captain Chase*? You're not in the Army, are you?"

"That's confidential information."

"You can trust me."

"Not with sensitive info."

"Pretty please?"

"Let's just say I'm well-trained in firing my load."

I giggle again at his stupid comment. Sober me would never put up with a pun like that.

But I'm not sober me.

I step up on my tippy toes, still nowhere near his height. I drunkenly lean forward and kiss him slowly on his lips. Captain Chase kisses me back. His thick arms reach around me and pull me in tighter. I'm glad he's got me because my drunk-ass was going to fall over at any moment.

I bite at his full lips and he's equally aggressive back. It's like I'm a wild animal. I'm overcome with this primal urge to fuck his brains out right here, right now.

I simply can't stop myself.

I honestly don't know what's come over me. This is the total opposite of who I am. I'm the uptight receptionist. The rich daddy's girl. *Little Miss Stuck-Up.* And yet here I am trying to devour a man twice my size. Maybe it's to do with the alcohol flowing freely through my veins, or maybe it has to do with something deep inside me. Something natural that's only unleashed when a horny woman meets a hot-blooded man at the peak of his prime. Something that stretches back thousands of years of evolution.

It doesn't matter. All that's important is that I want him. Right. Now.

As if sensing my uncontrollable desire, Captain Chase pulls me up off the ground and rests me on top of the bathroom sink.

We still kiss as I feel one of his hands let go of me. His fingers travel down the side of my dress, tenderly grazing my skin in a way that makes me shiver with excitement until his hand reaches that sweet spot between my legs.

I've never felt anything like this for a very, *very* long time.

He breaks off the kiss.

And that sends me into overdrive.

"Oh, Captain Chase," I groan.

"Call me Chase. Just Chase," he says.

"Don't stop kissing me, Chase."

"I wouldn't dream of it."

I gasp. "Oh God, what am I doing?" I ask out loud to no one in particular.

*I really don't know what the hell I'm doing.*

"You want me to do this, *Anna*?"

The gruff way he says my name makes me melt inside.

"Do whatever you want, Chase. Just as long as you do something to me right now."

"Yes, ma'am."

I groan again as two of his fingers penetrate me. That's when I realize how wet I am. This stripper really knows how to get the juices flowing in a woman, that's for sure. I glance down at his body. At his perfectly formed abs. At his cock that's standing upright. He's so incredibly hard for me.

I moan as his fingers work magic inside of me. He pulls them out to gently caress my clit, and it's like a thousand fireworks explode in my belly. I feel him all over.

I watch him through tear-soaked eyes as he leans over me and whispers into my ear. "I want to fuck you, Anna."

I nod my head and bite my lip in response. I can't even say anything. This is already too much.

He pulls my panties away. As I balance on top of the sink, he reaches down to a drawer below and produces a condom wrapper.

"Stop," I moan. "Not yet."

Chase, not knowing what I'm about to do, stands still.

*I know exactly what I'm doing.*

25

I take his erect cock in my hand and start to play with it. It's so thick my fingers barely wrap around it. I stare at Chase as his eyes rolls to the back of his head. His gorgeous mouth hangs open. I'm glad to be able to make him *feel* something for a change.

I bring him to the point of climax. His body shakes. His cock vibrates between my fingers.

And only then do I allow him to enter me.

He rips apart the condom packet and slides it on his massive cock. He must get those condoms in *extra-large* size.

I can't believe that thick shaft is going to enter me. It's dripping with pre-cum.

But it does.

And my eyes go wide.

I didn't want to come into the strip club tonight.

And now I'm ending the night by getting fucked backstage.

# 3

*ANNA*

I REALLY, really want to be sick.

Little known fact here, but did you know hangovers are tough? Because they *freaking* are.

"I'm looking for Mr. Dunn's office."

I raise my heavy head, currently swimming in night-old champagne, and look up from the reception desk at the man in the business attire standing in front of me.

What is it that Tom Cruise says about champagne in *Cocktail?*

*Perfume going in, sewage going out.*

Yep. Feels like it.

And right now, I feel my face drooping as I attempt to speak to the businessman from behind the desk. "Huh?"

He blinks at me, obviously catching onto the fact that I am either severely hungover or that I need to be in a psych ward.

"Can you show me the way to Mr. Dunn's office? I have an appointment with him."

*Oh, right.*

I'm meant to be doing my job. That little thing.

I lift my shaking arm in the right direction.

"Down the hall and to the right. It's the second office."

"Uh, thanks."

The man scurries away from me before I can projectile vomit over him. I don't blame him. I do feel like I am actually really close to spewing forth my guts.

I want to be sick and my head hurts like hell.

This is why I don't drink often. I get the *worst* hangovers.

An email notification pops up on the computer screen in front of me, but I totally ignore it. Instead, I reach for my takeaway cup of coffee – my third one today – and try to drink from it. The cup's empty. I've already drunk it all.

*Great.*

That's a disappointment.

Why did I even turn up to work today? Last night was an absolute mess. I woke up this morning in the bathroom of my apartment, leaning over the toilet bowl in a half-hearted attempt to throw up. And it seems like it's only gotten worse from there.

In the taxi on my way to work, the events of last night slowly dawned on me in little snippets, and I started to freak out in the car. The strip club. Going on stage. Drinking my bodyweight in champagne. My pitiful endeavor to locate a bathroom. Then remembering, worst of all, making my way backstage, where naked Captain Chase found me peeing in his dressing room.

And then the hot, filthy sex session we had in his private bathroom.

*What in the actual hell came over me?*

Why did I do that?

From then on, things get a little rocky. I remember we

had a drink together after I had the most powerful orgasm of my life.

*Ha, me and a male stripper shared a drink together.*

Then I can kind of remember him calling a cab for me. Then me going home. I can recall snippets of being in the taxi on the way back to mine, replying to a dozen messages from Erin asking where the fuck I was.

Then the next thing I remember is waking up in my bathroom, still wearing the same dress from the night before.

*What a mess you are, Anna.*

Last night had been, without a doubt, the *craziest* night of my life.

So not like me at all.

And now I'm sitting on my ass behind the reception desk at work, on the top level of my dad's company, trying not to throw up.

*One thing's for sure. I'm never doing last night ever again.*

My spinning head lowers to the desk again. I just want to sleep it off.

I pull out my phone. Maybe scrolling through Instagram will keep me from nodding off. Maybe being a sleeping receptionist outside the office of one of the most powerful and richest CEOs in the state - let alone the same man being my *father* - is not very good for my career prospects. Even I am smart enough to realize that.

My thumb flicks through the endless array of photos on my phone. My feed is filled with photos of my rich friends zooming around luxury locations. London. Paris. Tropical paradises. So many of my high school friends, all twenty-two years old like me, are already married to some dude who owns property on every continent. Some already have kids. When you're a female of wealthy stock, like I am, it seems like your one goal in life is to snap up some successful guy. Make sure you do it as young as possible and then your mission is to start producing babies. It's almost an abnormality in my high school friendship group that I'm not married, or even have a boyfriend. I guess I'm not really built for that, at least *not* just yet.

Bored with scrolling through vacation photos of the rich and famous, I search for the few contemporary painters I follow. I check through images of their latest creations on Instagram. Forget about luxury tropical resorts; this is much more my style. Painting. Artwork. I love it. And seeing all the beautiful art rushing past on my phone makes me feel incredibly guilty.

I would do anything to be back home, right now, painting, instead of being a receptionist to my billionaire father. Extremely hungover.

An advertisement pops up on my feed as I scroll through. It's for a painting course. Instagram must keep a track of what I'm interested in.

A painting course, though?

*I could do that.*

That would be the dream…

"What's up?"

I'm shocked by the sudden appearance of my best friend springing next to my shoulder.

"Erin! Don't scare me like that," I squeal in surprise, quickly locking my phone and chucking it onto the desk. My love of painting is a secret I keep from everyone. I don't know why, but I feel embarrassed revealing such a random passion to even my best friend.

"Where were you last night?" Erin asks, sitting down in the receptionist chair next to me. "You completely disappeared on us."

My best friend also works as a receptionist on the same

level as me. I'm on the main general desk by the elevators and she works privately for one of the Vice Presidents of the company.

I sigh. "I was exhausted. I just wanted to get home."

I don't want to tell her what really happened. No way. I would never hear the end of it, and I really don't feel like going over every sordid detail of that steamy sex I had with Captain Chase backstage. I want to completely forget that whole experience.

"No surprise there, what that guy did to you on stage would be pretty exhausting," Erin laughs. How can she appear fresh as a daisy when she probably drank more than I did? Practice, probably. "Everyone can't shut up about how funny it was.

"I'm the talk of the town this morning, I guess."

"You! On Stage! Even Daria couldn't contain herself. It was hilarious. You had fun, right?"

"Yep. Lots of fun."

I want to throw up.

"That Captain Chase guy was *such* a hunk, wasn't he? All those delicious muscles. What I would do for a single night with him."

"Yep."

"Wouldn't you agree, Anna?"

"He'll be alright, I guess."

God, I hate lying.

Erin catches on to my hungover condition. I don't know what gives it away, my sunken eyes or my patchy pale skin? Either way, there are enough clues to put two and two together.

"Oh, right. Had a bit too much to drink?"

"Yep."

She elbows me in the ribs, which doesn't help things at all. It just makes me want to throw up even more.

"Push through it. I'll shout you lunch, if you like. A big calorie-stuffed meal will do you wonders. Lots of carbs."

"I can't even think about food right now," I groan.

One of the Vice Presidents of the company, a pasty guy named Wayne, pokes his head around the corner. "Erin," he calls.

"Coming," she replies. She turns to me and rolls her eyes. "Gotta run. See you at lunch, yeah?"

I groan again, the champagne still swiveling around my head. "Sure."

I watch her as she merrily skips off down the hall towards Wayne. I honestly don't know where she gets all the energy after last night. She stops and turns before she's out of sight. "Oh, your dad wants to see you now," she calls.

"What? Dad?"

She waits until *now* to drop this information.

"Yep," she replies. "He just walked past my desk and told me to get you."

"Um. Right. Thanks."

Dad wants to see me now?

*Why?*

* * *

MR. JENSEN.

That's the name on his door. And even though it's my name, it still terrifies me every time I see it.

Dad has the biggest office in the skyscraper. It basically takes up the entire level at the top of the building. A big private office space and a whole load of conference rooms.

I work just one level below, so it doesn't take me long to get up there. Even so, I take my time to check myself out in the bathroom. Apply some more makeup. Try to look as presentable as I can.

I can't go visit my dad looking like the most hungover person in the country on a Monday morning.

Outside his door, I take in a deep breath before I knock.

"Come in."

I step into his office.

"Hi, Dad."

Mr. Jensen stands behind his desk. His eyes widen as I walk in and he approaches me for a kiss on the cheek. People like to say we look similar, but I don't see the resemblance. I reckon I look more like my mom.

His office looks out over the city. The walls around the room are made of glass. We're one of the tallest skyscrapers in the entire state. The view from the building is to die for, and Dad has the best one in here.

My dad is the typical billionaire CEO. Straight out of the movies. That George Clooney silver fox handsomeness. Expensive tailored suits from Milan and London. The best straight white teeth money can buy. His authority, all through my life, can only be superseded by the Almighty Himself. Dad is the ruler of the kingdom. Always has been.

And so I guess that makes me the spoiled princess.

"Hello, sweetheart," he says. "Please take a seat."

"Why do you want to see me?" I ask as I nervously place my ass on the leather chair facing his desk. Dad takes his position in his giant chair.

"A father can't see his daughter for no reason?" he asks me, his eyes piercing into my soul. I don't reply, letting him continue. "Well, there is something I'll like to talk about."

*Of course.* There's always a reason why Dad wants to see me. When you're as rich as he is, our family operates *slightly* differently from your average American family. Birthday parties as a kid were accompanied by armed security. Dad driving me to school was more like riding in the back of a presidential motorcade of blacked-out limousines.

"What do you want to talk about?" I ask.

Dad sighs and unbuttons his jacket. "It's to do with your future, Anna."

"My future?"

"Yes. Look, this is pretty strange to talk about, so I'll get straight to the point," Dad says, scratching his chin. "Marriage, Anna. It's time for you to consider a boyfriend."

I blink.

*A boyfriend? Marriage?*

Yeah, pretty strange to talk about. Where is all this coming from?

"Marriage?"

"Yes. It's about time for you to start considering your options."

"I'm only twenty-two, Dad."

"All the more reason to start thinking about this."

"Isn't this something that happens a bit more... *naturally*?" I ask, looking around the massive office. "Rather than decided in a conference room?"

I'm not one to usually argue with my father, but this needs to be straightened out.

"I know it is something *awkward* to discuss," my father continues. "But you need to start seriously considering this."

"What about dates? Dating? Getting to know people?"

He waves his hand as if batting away a fly. "Sure. There'll be *dates*. But you need is to get married as soon as possible."

"And how long a timeframe are we talking about here?" I ask.

Dad nonchalantly scratches his chin again as if this is a perfectly normal conversation to have with your adult daughter. "I would say no longer than a year."

"A *year*?"

"Well, ideally less than that."

"Just one year to get married?"

"Yes."

"And what about love?"

It feels ridiculous even saying it.

Dad chuckles as if I was talking about dragons or something else imaginary. "We're discussing marriage here, Anna. Not love. Love is for street bums. Love is for the regular people, not for people like us. Marriage is for stability. That's what is important for people like you and me, Anna. You need to get married, sweetheart. To a suitable man. And it needs to be soon."

I feel completely shut down. I know it's my time to shut up now because Dad is on one of his lectures, and the man isn't used to people interrupting him in mid-flow. I'm wise enough not to stop him whilst he's on a roll.

"Love isn't useful when you can't pay for a roof over your head," Dad continues. "You need to find a decent, well-bred young man. Start your own family. I can't have you being my receptionist for the next fifty years, can't I?"

I gulp.

"So, what are you suggesting?"

"I'm glad you ask that," Dad replies, leaning forward. "Because someone is interested in you already, and I think he might be a good match for you."

"You've found someone already?"

"How about you go on a date with him and see what he's like? I've spoken to him about this and he's very keen to meet you, and I'm very keen to put you two together."

It's like all my dreams of independence fall away in front of my eyes in real-time as Dad speaks. I should've known this day was coming for a long while. This is what I've been groomed for since birth. This is the price you pay for being the only daughter of one of the richest CEOs in the state.

My future dreams seem to shrivel away the more Dad mentions this guy. My freedom. Painting. All in the service of me getting married and pumping out babies.

"Who?" I ask timidly, and my dad smiles.

"He's here now. He's standing outside the door. I'll introduce you."

# 4

SIX MONTHS LATER

*ANNA*

I TAKE another sip of the expensive French white wine and look out over the view, completely blanking out what my boyfriend is telling me. From the lavish rooftop restaurant, I can see the whole city arrayed below me. It's night, and all the little lights of the city sparkle like stars. In the distance, I can spot my family's skyscraper, just a few maintenance lights on inside the tall building. Everyone's gone home except for a few cleaners.

The only reason I live in the city is simply because my father is based here. There's never been another option for me to live anywhere else. It was always assumed I would stay close to my family home, close to the headquarters of the family business. There's a whole world out there to discover and I just live here.

And it's pretty boring.

Maybe one day I'll escape. See the world on my own terms.

*Yeah, a girl can wish.*

"Are you listening to me?"

*Whoops.*

I've totally forgotten about my boyfriend. I quickly flick my focus away from the rooftop bar's view and back onto the man sitting opposite me.

"Sorry," I murmur. "Long day."

Angus Allen looks smartly dressed in his expensively tailored suit; a shiny new Rolex wrapped around his wrist. He sighs at me, his perfectly plucked brows furrowing as if I'd committed a criminal offense by zoning out whilst he was talking about his stock portfolio for the millionth time. I don't mean to be rude, but the varying price of the international stock market is pretty low on my interest list, and he knows that. Sometimes I think he just talks at me as if I'm a doll to simply nod along and indulge him.

"Doesn't matter," he says, waving his hand. He reaches for his own wine glass. "Let's talk about something else."

"Sure," I reply, stilted.

"Let's talk about us."

*Oh no.*

Before he can continue, he's interrupted by the waiter.

"Ready to order?"

Angus pouts at the man, annoyed at being stopped mid-conversation. "I'll have the Wagyu beef. Medium. And a bottle of your Burgundy."

The waiter turns to me. "And for you, Ma'am?"

Before I can answer, Angus speaks for me. "The lady will have the seafood linguine and another glass of white."

"Very good."

I *would* be shocked that Angus ordered on my behalf without even asking me *if* it wasn't such a normal occurrence.

I keep my mouth shut. No point in having an argument now in the middle of dinner.

Instead, I take another sip of my white wine to wash away my frustration.

The rooftop restaurant is one of the best in the city. It sits on top of the most luxurious hotel in the state. Some people would treat this expensive place as a once-a-year treat, but for Angus and me, it's a regular weekend haunt.

Angus leans forward over the table. "So, as I was saying before I was rudely interrupted," he continues. "Let's talk about us."

"Okay, what is it?"

He reaches out and takes my hand in his. He strokes my fingers as he speaks.

"It's been six months since we've been together. Actually, as of tonight, it's been *exactly* six months since our first date."

"It has."

Angus smiles. "I remember when your dad introduced us in his office."

"Me too."

"I'm telling you, Anna, it was love at first sight."

"It was for me."

Oh, I remember exactly when Dad called Angus into his office.

*My boy, have you met my daughter, Anna?*

"The sly bastard, your old man knew what he was doing. He knew how compatible we are. You, his daughter, and me, one of the Vice Presidents at Jensen. He's a smart man, that Mr. Jensen."

"I'm a bit biased, but he sure is."

Angus, being one of the rising stars at my father's company, definitely played a part in why Dad brought us together. I couldn't dare say no to our first date, and I certainly couldn't say no a week later when Angus asked me to be his girlfriend. I completely understand why Dad was so eager to pair us up. On paper, we are a perfect match. Both privately educated at two of the best schools in the country, both with wealthy parents, Angus being a successful young businessman at the company, and attractive as well. We're like a real-life Daisy and Tom Buchanan out of *The Great Gatsby*. The elite of elite couples.

"Which brings me to tonight, and why we're here," Angus continues.

"I thought we're here for dinner," I reply, and Angus laughs. He squeezes my hand tighter.

"It's more than that, Anna. I want to celebrate six months of being together. Six glorious months. Six months that have changed my life."

"And changed mine."

"Which is why I want to do this." And before I know it, Angus launches himself out of his seat and is kneeling down on the ground next to my chair.

*Oh my god.*

This can't be happening.

But it is.

He raises his hands up to me. He's holding a little black box open, and inside the box is a diamond ring.

What can only be described as an *engagement ring*.

*He's really doing this? Here? Now?*

I start to shake. My mouth hangs open. The entire restaurant falls silent.

"I've spoken to your father," Angus continues, his voice quivering. He's never nervous like this. "I've asked him this question, and he's given me his approval. Anna Jensen, will you marry me?"

The first thing that comes to mind isn't the last six months of being together with Angus, or what our wedding will be, or what our kids will look like, or even what our future together could hold. No. The first thing that comes to my mind is Dad's words to me from six months ago.

*We're discussing marriage here, Anna. Not love. Love is for street bums. Love is for the regular people, not for people like us. Marriage is for stability. That's what is important for people like you and I, Anna. You need to get married, sweetheart. To a suitable man. And it needs to be soon.*

Those words have not left my head since. They are burned into my soul.

Angus is the epitome of the *suitable* man my father wants me to marry. I mean, he's already given Angus his seal of approval. This is what I've been brought up to do. This moment, at this restaurant, is what my whole life has been geared towards.

And I know I can only say one thing.

"Yes."

Angus smiles, and the entire restaurant - waiters and kitchen - erupts into enthusiastic applause.

My new fiancé stands and slides the ring onto my finger. My heart wants to burst out of my chest. I smile along with him, but I know it's fake. It's all for show.

Truth be told, I don't know what the *hell* I'm doing. I feel like I've been forced into this.

As everyone in the restaurant applauds, I don't feel like myself. I feel like I'm a ghostly spectator looking down at this, at someone else called Anna Jensen saying yes to Angus Allen. I don't want this to be real. It's all happening so fast. Way too fast.

As our waiter brings over the best champagne to celebrate, Angus leans over and whispers into my ear. "I knew you'd say yes. I've booked the best suite in the hotel below. Let's spend the night here."

And, like the proposal, I know I can't say no.

# 5

*ANNA*

WELL. That was boring sex.

I lie in bed after Angus falls asleep, unable to drift off. My fiancé lies next to me, snoring. His body gently rises and falls with each guttural sound coming from his nose.

I sigh and look up at the ceiling of the hotel suite. A silver chandelier hangs above us.

The best hotel room in the city.

*How can he go straight to sleep after such impassionate lovemaking?*

I shake my head. I'm just complaining, my head's full of negative energy. I should stop thinking like this.

But it's true.

That truly was uninspiring sex.

You would think the passion immediately after a proposal should be one of the most intense nights of your life. And, sure, everything was set up to go that way. The luxury hotel suite. The bottle of champagne in an ice bucket. The rose petals on the massive bed.

But it didn't turn out that way.

It was more like a David Attenborough documentary where Angus was simply an elephant mounting the female in the African wilds. Pure biology. No *emotion*. Just going through the motions.

For one single minute.

Look, I don't ask for much, but I expect that maybe I should feel fulfilled at least once in the bedroom. At the very least on the night of my engagement. That's all I'm asking for.

*Yeah, you really are complaining whilst you lie in a luxury bed. Get a hold of yourself, Anna.*

Angus snores again and turns away from me. He takes most of the bedsheets with him.

The last six months with Angus have been charmless, at least in the bedroom. He's handsome, though. Smart. Successful. Sure, we're a good match *on paper*, but in the bedroom there's simply no spark.

And I can't help thinking that maybe it has nothing to do with my new fiancé.

That maybe it's me.

My mind drifts back to a time before my first date with Angus, to a memory I've kept locked away in the back of my mind. The memory of that crazy night in the strip club. The one time I was uncharacteristically spontaneous and actually had a lot of fun.

That passionate night with so-called Captain Chase.

As I lie here in the hotel bed next to Angus, my right hand slowly creeps down the length of my body as I think back on that drunk-fueled night. Everything comes back to me in sensual waves. The illicit touching in the dressing room bathroom. The stripper's oiled-up muscles. The way his green eyes stared at me with that pure, animalistic lust. His smirk. His dimples.

Under the silk bedcovers, my hand reaches for my pussy. It's wet. Soaking wet. I begin to play with myself as memories of that intense night flood my body.

I close my eyes.

*The way he lifted me up onto the bathroom sink as if I weighed nothing.*

My fingers on my clit rub faster.

*The way he tenderly touched me. Him sliding his thick fingers into my soft entrance. How I moaned.*

My body shakes.

*That hunk of a man who knew how to make me squirm.*

I feel him again as if he's here beside me. I feel him right in my core.

I let out a soft gasp as I bring myself to orgasm on the bed. I try not to make a sound, but it's incredibly difficult.

*That was better than sex with my fiancé.*

I lie still, panting.

Next to me, Angus stirs. I'm suddenly brought back to reality. My fiancé turns over to face me.

I freeze.

*What the fuck am I doing? This? Next to sleeping Angus?*

My breathing's shallow.

I risk a quick glance over at him. He's still completely knocked out.

*Thank God.*

That would be hard to explain to him. How can you even begin to explain your hand deep in your panties in the middle of the night?

*You're insane, Anna.*

I pull myself out of the bed gently as to not wake up my unconscious fiancé. I stagger across the immense room to the en-suite. I turn the light on and stand in front of the sink, looking at my frazzled reflection in the mirror.

*You really are crazy, Anna. Complaining in your head about your new fiancé. Touching yourself over an insane drunk experience you had months ago.*

I tut at myself, thinking of how stupid I am. I wash my hands in the golden sink as if I'm trying to wipe all the guilt away down the drain.

My looks will be gone one day, and then I'll just be another receptionist. It's just what Dad had said. If I don't follow through with Angus, despite our problems, then I'll end up as another marriage-less rich daddy's girl.

All through high school, in my elite private school, I was bottom of the class in academic work. I would get teased about it by the other rich girls. Math and science weren't for me, not for the way my brain works. But *art*, that was *my* thing. I didn't care what the other girls thought; I was gifted in painting.

I even dreamed at one point about going pro.

But that was a long time ago, a time before I learned how the real world works and my destined place in it. It was silly of me to ever even consider painting as a career when I have the life I have.

Dad was right. I have to get married, and Angus is by far the best fit for me.

There's a quiet knock on the bathroom door. I turn off the tap and turn around.

Angus stands in the doorway, his eyes half-closed. He's just woken up.

"Sorry, did I wake you?" I ask tentatively.

"Kinda," he replies groggily. He takes a step into the bathroom towards me. He wraps his arms around my shoulders from behind, cuddling me close. We stand here on the cold marble flooring and look at ourselves in the large bathroom mirror for a moment. Angus leans over my shoulder. "What you doing?" he asks.

"Just washing my hands and face. I can't sleep."

"Right."

"Sorry for waking you up," I say softly.

There's another long pause as we both continue staring at our reflection.

"It's no problem," Angus eventually replies.

"I can't believe we're going to get married," I say with a slight smile.

"Me too."

"It's going to be magical. Thank you for doing it in such an amazing way."

"I was thinking about it," Angus says. "And I was thinking about our living arrangements."

"Oh yeah?"

"I was thinking about how we live separately at the moment. Well, now that we're engaged, how about you move into my apartment?"

I nod. "Okay."

It was inevitable this was going to happen.

Angus chuckles. "It'll allow me to keep a close eye on you. Keep you out of trouble," he says. "How about you get your stuff into mine tomorrow? I've got a guy who I can call to collect your things immediately."

"Maybe let's not rush into this so quickly," I reply hesitatingly. "It's a big deal living together."

"But we're engaged now, babe."

I know I can't win this.

As my new fiancé holds me from behind, I take a look at my ring in the mirror. My big diamond engagement ring.

*Everything's moving so fast.*

All of this in six months.

But what would Dad say to my doubts? What would my family think? I *should* move into his place. I understand how it's the right thing to do. We are an engaged couple, after all. This is what's supposed to happen.

*So why am I full of doubts?*

As I stand here in the bathroom with Angus's arms around me, I mull over my future name. Repeating it over and over in my head.

*Anna Allen. Anna Allen. Anna Allen.*

Does it even have a nice ring to it? I don't even know anymore.

Maybe everyone has doubts like this. Maybe I'm just a little bit crazy. Maybe I'm just a little bit too independent-minded for my own good. Maybe I should just shut my mouth and go through with this all and stop all this incessant complaining in my head.

"So?" Angus asks.

There's only one answer I can say to my future husband.

"Okay, sure. Whatever's best for you. I'm happy to move in tomorrow if you want to give your guy a call."

"Perfect." Angus smiles. "I love you, babe."

"I love you too," I reply softly.

And now I know it's too late to back out now.

# 6

## CHASE

I JUMP off the stage to the screams of a hundred women.

*Beautiful.*

I smile to myself as I head backstage, away from all the noise and lights, and back into the quiet of my dressing room.

*What a show that was.*

I think I made a couple of the females in the audience squirt in their pants. At least it looked like they did. Always a good sign of a good show.

I throw off the tight leather BDSM gear I've been wearing on stage in exchange for my standard white t-shirt and leather jacket. I turn and inspect myself in the dressing room mirror. Harsh years on the road like this, jumping relentlessly from strip club to strip club, still haven't revealed themselves on my twenty-four-year-old face. I'm still looking as fresh as the day I started on this crazy, unreliable career at sixteen.

*Damn, boy, if the show tonight's anything to go by, you've still got it.*

Indeed, I do. In spades. I've still got a lotta years left in this stripping game.

Gathering my wallet and keys, I head out of my dressing room and into the office next door.

"Time to collect my winnings, Toby," I say as I enter Xstasy's office with my usual swagger. The manager of the club sits behind his desk, piles of cash and paperwork stacked around him. The man's a vulture, always trying to take a little extra off the top each night from everyone who works here, but I like him nonetheless. And he likes me.

I fall into the chair opposite Toby with my trademark louche lean and stare at the manager from across the desk.

"What's the number?" I ask smugly. I snatch a bar of Toby's chewing gum from the corner of his desk and lob one into my mouth. I start to chew on it. Loudly.

Xstasy's manager tuts at me and chucks over a roll of bills in my direction. I catch it with one hand. "Two hundred," he says.

"Two hundred? That's nothing."

"That's what's been brought in tonight."

I roll my eyes.

"Come on, Toby. Surely there's more."

"Nope."

I stare him down. "What are you hiding up your sleeve, Toby? You can fool all the other guys in here, but me? No. I wasn't born yesterday. I'm onto you."

The manager sighs. "Alright, I can throw you a little extra. Just don't tell the other guys." He chucks another bill at me reluctantly.

I look down at it.

"Fifty?"

"Yep."

"Bullshit."

Toby shrugs. "It's been a slow night."

"I've seen the crowd out there, Toby. It isn't a slow night."

"I've also seen you scoring free drinks at the bar ever since you've started here. This works both ways."

I chuckle. "Fair enough." I pull myself out of the chair and head towards the door. "But I've got my eye on you, Toby."

I reach the door. "Hey, Chase."

I turn. "Yeah?"

"Good show tonight," Toby says.

"Good shows don't pay rent," I reply, walking out of there.

The bar at Xstasy is at the far back of the club, located along the opposite wall to the stage. The line of stools along the bar counter is very familiar to me. I wander over there and take a seat at the far corner, away from any wandering eyes of drunk patrons looking for one of the guys on stage.

I keep a low profile and nod at Stacy, Xstasy's bartender. She sidles up to me, already popping open a beer. She knows what I like before I even order.

"The show tonight was *great*, handsome," she says as she slides the beer down the counter towards my waiting hand.

"You think?" I reply. Stacy leans over the bar, tantalizingly revealing her impressive rack.

"Oh yes. You were sublime."

Despite the high levels of tension between us, Stacy and I have never fucked, and nor will we. I maintain a strict code since I started this career. I've learned it - often the hard way - in all my years of stripping.

And guess what my top rule is?

*Never fuck your co-workers.*

Never *ever*.

No matter how hot and willing they may be, you just don't go there. Period.

You have to be careful with where you put your dick, especially in this business.

I have a lot of rules that I religiously stick to when it comes to this stripping game, and they haven't got me into trouble. Yet.

"Thanks, Stacy."

"You're welcome, stud."

She gives me a wink and saunters away. What a tease. She'll definitely want to get into my pants. If only my rules weren't against it...

Hey, at least she gives me free drinks, though.

I take a sip of the nice cold beer and settle onto the bar stool. I keep my focus away from the stage. I can tell from the stereotypical jungle music going on around me that Ryan's performing his whole *Tarzan* routine. I reckon it's a bit old and stale, but the crowd is evidently lapping it up, judging from the screams alone. Good for him.

Me, on the other hand? I like to keep my routines fresh.

My eyes flitter over to the other side of Xstasy's bar. There's a bunch of girls, presumably on a bachelorette night, drowning a line of shots. I smile at their loud display. At the rate they're going, they're gonna be passed out on the floor in half an hour.

*Thank god I don't work security. I don't want to deal with the aftermath of a messy bachelorette night.*

One of the girls is not partaking in the shots. She's the only one not squealing like a drunk pig.

And she's giving me the *eye*.

Oh, I know the *eye*. Look, I'm a male stripper; I instantly know when a girl is giving me the full-on *fuck me* glare. I know when a woman's entire body is pushing her onto me. As a pro, it isn't hard to see when a girl is practically drooling for you, when she is practically *begging* for you to come over and fuck her. Of course, they never say it themselves. Women want a man to approach them out of his own free will.

And I'm that kind of man.

I take another sip of beer. Yep, I feel her eyes all over me.

*Fuck it. Let's do this.*

I turn back towards her, beckoning her to me with a finger.

She comes. Willingly. Eagerly. Across the bar.

My cock hardens. I feel it press into my jeans. I always love this bit.

She sashays over to the barstool next to mine. She's got nice, long, black hair. She's a stunner.

"Hi," I say.

"Hello," she replies.

I nod at the stool. "Take a seat."

"Thank you." She does. I shoot a quick glance at her perky ass. It's *very* good.

I offer out my hand. "Chase."

She giggles. "Don't you mean *Captain Chase*?"

A chuckle escapes my lips. "Ah, so you watched the show, huh?"

"I might have," she replies, biting her plump lower lip. It's very inviting. "And I might have enjoyed it."

"Oh, I see."

She shakes my hand. "Alice."

"What do you want to drink, Alice?" I ask, pointing at the bar. "I can get you anything you want."

"Oh," she replies, flicking her head back at the loud bachelorette party. "I'm not drinking tonight. I'm the responsible one."

"Right. Designated driver?"

She eyes my body up and down.

"Yeah, something like that."

"And are you lot having a good time?"

"What do you think?"

I smile. I see her melt at my dimples. I always get them with my dimples.

"You're right. I'm here. Of course you're having a good time."

She giggles. Again. "You're cocky, Captain Chase. I like it."

The *heat* coming from this chick. It's unbearable. We're going to have to do something about this tension, and fast.

"Well, it's a shame I can't buy you a drink, Alice."

"Oh, I may not be drinking," she says, winking. "But I am so very, very *thirsty*."

It doesn't take a veteran male stripper to know what that means.

Oh yeah, about my rules of stripping? There's not one about fucking a woman who comes up to you after a show.

In fact, sleeping with the customer is actively *encouraged*.

*And the customer is always right.*

\* \* \*

I should've guessed it. Alice is a rich girl.

Her place screams it. A nice apartment in the nice end of town. I always seem to attract the high-powered ones.

The rich ones love a filthy stripper for a good night.

Alice ditched her bachelorette party and all her friends and took me back to mine. The easy way she just dumped the bride-to-be was pretty impressive. Even I have to admit, ditching your friends to get some dick is pretty brutal. But, working at Xstasy, I've seen it all before. There must be something to do with one of your friends imminently getting married that sends women's horniness drives into overtime.

*Hey, I ain't complaining, though.*

Another gem of wisdom I've found out is that rich girls are absolutely *dirty* in bed. Like, really fucking *gasping* for it rough and ready. It must have to do with the fact they have to keep it all together most of the day. The bedroom is their one escape, the one time they can let a man use them and abuse them.

And Alice is no exception.

We fuck deep into the early morning until we roll over, exhausted. I pride myself on my stamina - I'm pretty damn good at maintaining it all together in bed - but this Alice chick's somehow taken it all out of me.

She falls asleep whilst I still gather my breath.

*Wow.*

I've lost count of how many girls I've fucked a long, long time ago.

I stare up at her apartment ceiling from the middle of her bed.

*Time for me to leave.*

I'm not a cuddler. No sir.

I roll out of bed. She doesn't wake, thank God. I cautiously make my way around her apartment, gathering all my items of clothing that lie scattered everywhere because of the passionate mess we've made. By the look of things, I think we somehow fucked in all four corners of her room. I don't even remember what we did; I was too busy pulling her hair and biting her neck to worry about where exactly we were in her place.

*Right. I think that's everything.*

As I make my way to her bedroom door, she stirs and moans towards me.

"Where are you going?" she asks softly from the bed, half-asleep.

I've learned the hard way there's no point in lying to a woman. They always find out you're not telling the truth.

"I'm leaving," I reply in a whisper.

"Stay the night."

I shrug. "That's not really my style."

"Oh." Her voice is brimming with rejection and sadness. "How about you give me your number?"

"As great as this was, Anna, I think this is a one-time thing. We come from two *very* different worlds."

"Oh."

"Trust me, in the sober morning you'll realize that too. It's been fun. This can always be that one fun night you had with that stripper you met at the bar."

"It was fun."

"Yeah," I reply. "It was fun."

I get out of there before she can fully come to her senses. I don't want to deal with an argument at this time of the night.

As I head down the hallway to her lavish apartment's front door, I pass by a stand with a row of framed photos on it. My eyes catch a glimpse of her. Next to a man. She's in a white dress.

Now I'm really glad I didn't give her my number.

*She's married?*

Fuck.

The stand is full of wedding photos of her and this poor dude. She must've removed her ring before she went to the club tonight. Sneaky.

*Great.*

This has happened to me a couple of times before. A

married woman using me for sex is nothing new, but it still makes me angry.

Look, I may be *very* sexually liberated compared to your average American, but I still fucking hate cheaters. That's very much not my style at all.

And tonight Alice used me as a fantasy.

*Fuck you, Chase. You were so keen to jump into her bed that you didn't even consider whether she was just going to use you.*

Oh well, it was still a fun night. Despite her being a cheating bastard.

But all fantasies must end.

I leave her apartment, and I don't care about slamming her front door shut with a bang on the way out.

## 7

*CHASE*

God, I love the sound of my motorcycle. The thing produces such a guttural noise every time I rev it up. Something medieval comes out of it.

My motorcycle is a deep growling beast of a machine, and I love it.

Being on the back of it makes me feel alive in ways that warm even my cold playboy heart. The thing is my pride and joy above everything else in my life. Perched on the back of the motorcycle behind its thick handlebars, with the wind blowing all around me, is exactly where I am supposed to be.

It's still dark when I drive into the trailer park just outside the city, my motorcycle groaning as I slow it down from the daredevil speeds I was gunning it on the highway. The morning sun hasn't made its first appearance on the horizon just yet, but I sense it must be soon. The birds are beginning to wake as I rev towards my trailer parked at the far end of the site; I can hear them chirping their morning birdsong as I pull to a stop outside my place. I turn off the ignition and dismount the motorcycle, breathing in the crisp fresh air, and I head inside my trailer.

Yeah, I live in a rented trailer. So what? People can judge me all they like, but I honestly don't give a fuck. The place is cheap, that's why I live here. And living cheap comes with plenty of bonuses. I'm not tied down, that's one. I can grab all my shit anytime I want and be a ghost in less than an hour. I can disappear entirely whenever I want to. I like that. I like my freedom to go where and do whatever I please. I'm not shackled to some overpriced mortgage.

The inside of the trailer reflects my nomad lifestyle. As a man on the road, I don't need much to survive. Just some clothes, my motorcycle, and my dancing skills. A simple life, just the way I want. My few shirts hang over my bed. All I need is my little kitchen. All I need are a few pots and pans, a couple of sets of cutlery, my phone, its charger, and not much else. Some chick I once brought home here said I was a *minimalist*. I didn't know the term, but that could be what I am. I dunno. I'm just living my life the way I want to, that's it.

No woman ties me down.

I'm a free man.

I head to the sink and pour myself a glass of water. I'm going to settle in, pull the curtains shut, and sleep until my next show tonight. A perfect day.

*Bang bang bang.*

There's a loud knocking at my trailer door.

I spin around in my tiny kitchen.

*Who the fuck's banging on my door so early in the morning?*

I spy my baseball bat perched by the front door. My hand twitches. I'm ready to use it if I have to.

*Bang bang bang.*

"Who is it?" I call.

There's a pause.

"You know who it is."

*Fuck.*

Yep. I know exactly who it is.

Brandi.

The manager of the trailer park, and there can only be one reason why she's banging on my door at this time. Screw her.

*Bang bang bang.*

And I know she isn't going away until I open up.

I reluctantly unlock the door a tiny bit.

"What is it?" I growl through the little opening. "It's early in the morning. What are you doing banging on my trailer like this?"

Even in the night's darkness, I can still make out Brandi's heavy and round figure. She's a big lady. Her thin hair is always tied in a ponytail. She's missing a few teeth. She's a cheap redneck trailer park manager, and she's certainly not known to be the most *pleasant* of human beings. I've been on the receiving end of her screeching and yelling plenty of times.

I think it's safe to say we don't get along.

"Don't play games with me, Chase. I saw you zoom in on your bike."

"Is that a crime? Should I get a lawyer? Do you think I'm going to jail?"

"Don't be such a smartass shit with me. You know why I'm here."

I shoot her a cocky smile. "Why? Because you're simply *charmed* by me? You can't get enough of my sexy body?"

She's very clearly not amused.

Brandi's got to be the only woman I've ever met on

whom my seduction tricks don't work. I've thrown the entire playboy book at her, but she's never responded positively at all to my charms. I would respect her stubborn stoicism if she wasn't such a bitch.

"You know what I'm here for. Rent." Her hand protrudes from her belly towards me. "Here. Now."

"I don't have it."

"Don't do this, Chase."

"I really don't."

And it's true. I was in some money problems when I first arrived at the trailer park over a year ago. And by money problems, I mean *no money*. Brandi only took me in so that she can demand extortionate interest on every month I couldn't pay. She's sucking me dry, the old bat, and I'm still slowly paying off the backlog. She doesn't relent. The trailer park manager likes to come around and threaten me like this every once in a while, but I don't pay attention to her.

And this time is no exception.

"I'll get you the rent when my next payment is due," I reply. "That's all I can promise."

"I should tear your place apart."

I shrug. "Sure, but you won't find anything except for some used condoms."

Brandi's lips curl into a snarl at my joke, but she's smart enough to know she isn't going to get any money out of me today.

"This is your last chance, Chase. The very last chance. Next time I'm bringing around my cousins. They'll knock some sense into you."

Yeah, I've seen her cousins.

Them coming around here wouldn't be a family picnic. They're less like a Thanksgiving gathering and more like an armed gang.

"Thanks for being such a darling," I reply to her sarcastically before locking the door closed on her sneer.

Despite my jokiness, I know I better take her threats seriously.

I sigh and close the trailer curtains, getting ready for bed.

Yep. I need money. And soon.

8

*ANNA*

REVEALING to all your friends and family that you're newly engaged seems to be a bigger deal than the actual proposal itself. This is when the real excitement happens. This is when it really does sink in that you're about to vow yourself to another person forever.

Which is what has led me here, to a lunch date with Erin, at a Mexican restaurant across the street from the skyscraper where we both work.

It was actually my idea to go out for lunch.

"Psst, Erin," I whispered to her from around the corner. It was the morning, and we were both meant to be at our desks working, but I had skillfully snuck across the hallway to speak to her.

My best friend raised her head from her computer screen. Her eyes widened at me. "What is it?" she asked, excited.

I hadn't told her yet about Angus's proposal. The only people who knew were our two families.

"You. Me. Lunch," I mouthed across the room.

I glanced behind me. Some dude walked past, but he didn't suspect I was not where I was supposed to be.

Erin clapped her hands together in enthusiastic agreement. I pointed to my phone, indicating I'll message her details before I slid back to my desk.

Erin, of course, was more than eager to come. She loves a good work lunch. Especially if there's an opportunity for booze to get involved.

It's the next day on from when Angus proposed to me on that rooftop restaurant and, in typical me fashion, I don't know how to tell my best friend the good news. On the other hand, letting my parents know what had happened was easy. All that took was a quick phone call. They already knew it was coming, as Angus had dramatically asked for Dad's permission just a few weeks ago, but even then, they took it like it was a good contract agreement. They reacted like the whole thing was inevitable. They seemed happier that I had actually accepted. Dad was already making plans on how to bring Angus in closer to the business operations as we spoke over the phone. It didn't feel like a parent being happy for their child; it was more like another company merger on Wall Street, all professional and formal. Not an ounce of emotion.

But I knew revealing it to Erin would be a completely different affair entirely.

I really don't want to draw it out, so I let her know nearly as soon as we took our seats in the Mexican restaurant whilst our waitress collected our water.

"I have something to tell you," I say to my best friend, practically whispering as to not create a scene.

Erin, with her sixth sense for these types of things, already had guessed what I was intending to tell her by the time I fitted the diamond ring on my hand and lifted it up for her to see.

"Oh. My. *God.*"

*Creating a public scene? Yep, we're not going to avoid that now.*

At the sight of the diamond, she opens her mouth and squeals. The entire restaurant turns to stare.

Typical Erin.

She doesn't care how loud she's being. She fusses and coos over the ring, completely enthralled by it.

"Oh, it's *gorgeous*. He must've spent a pretty penny or two on it."

"I think so."

"I love it, do you?"

I nod in agreement.

Then there's the machine-gun fire of the expected questions.

"How did it happen? What did he say? Tell me everything. Where was it? How did you react? Were you embarrassed? I bet you were embarrassed, Anna. Do you have a date? Where are you going to have it? What are your ideas for it? Do you know what designer you're going to wear? Who are you inviting?"

I laugh and shake my head at her. Erin is impossible to talk to when her mouth is rattling off at such speeds. To be honest, I'm happy that she's reacting in such a way. I needed some emotion after all my doubts and my parents' business-like phone-call. I spent last night completely in doubt of my decision to say yes, but seeing how excited she is makes me feel like I did the right thing.

"Okay," I reply to the giddy girl sitting opposite me. "I'm going to reply to all your questions, but first I need to ask *you* a question."

"What?"

"Will you be my maid of honor?"

Erin's face drops. Her eyes go wide. It's like she's been overcome with some mystical force lighting her up from the inside.

But before she can respond, our waitress returns.

"Are you girls ready to order?"

Erin turns to her, completely silent. She looks like a bomb about to go off. I'm worried she might explode at the poor waitress for daring to interrupt us in the middle of such an important conversation.

But instead, she asks the waitress one thing. "Your finest bottle of champagne. Two glasses, please."

*Oh.*

"I really shouldn't drink, Erin," I protest. "It's only lunch and I have a lot of work to do this afternoon."

"Hush you," Erin replies.

"I can't have a boozy lunch."

"You're getting married, Anna. Lighten up. Enjoy it."

"I really can't do this, Erin."

My best friend rolls her eyes at me before turning back to the waitress. "She's just got engaged and I'm going to be the maid of honor. She just told me. It's the best day of our lives. We'll definitely be needing that bottle of champagne."

I can't fight back. I'm completely powerless.

I laugh at my best friend, resigned.

*Screw it. I'm going to get drunk.*

The waitress returns with a bottle of bubbly, and the conversation flows along with the drink. I recount how last night unfolded. Erin sits across from me and laps up every detail, like it's a drug and she's an addict. She revels in it more than I do.

In terms of her own love life, she's always been perpetually single but *enjoying* it. Nearly every day in the office, I get to hear about the new guy she had around the night before. Sometimes it seems like Erin has slept in every rich bachelor's bed in the city. She and I are from similar backgrounds. Wealthy parents. Expensive elite private schools. The lot. No wonder we fitted so tightly together on our first day working together as receptionists. We're basically the same person, but also total opposites in personality. Erin's the outgoing, emotional, extroverted one, whilst I'm the steely, quiet, uptight one. Yin and yang. She's the jelly to my peanut butter.

I feel like I can tell her anything. Which means, once I'm a few glasses into the delicious champagne and I've lost a little bit of my famous self-control, I let my guard down and reveal things about last night that I would normally keep guarded.

"I do have some... *doubts*," I say quietly as I finish my third glass of champagne.

"Doubts?" Erin asks, taking another sip. We haven't even ordered food yet and we're already tipsy. "What do you mean?"

I pour myself another glass.

Here we go. Time to let it all out.

"I know Angus and I are perfect for each other. He ticks all the right boxes for me and everything about him is amazing. But there's a little seed of doubt burrowing in the back of my mind that we shouldn't go through with this."

Erin gasps. When she drinks, she somehow becomes even more dramatic than normal. "You mean *cancel* the wedding?"

I slowly nod. It feels super weird actually saying this out loud, but I guess the champagne is letting it all escape from the dark recesses of my heart. "Maybe."

Erin reaches out for me, taking my hand. "Look, I know Angus. We get on so well. I think you two are perfect for each other. I don't know where this is coming from."

"On paper, yes, we're perfect for each other. It's just... it's silly saying it."

"Say what?"

"I don't feel *sexy*."

Erin frowns at me. "You don't feel sexy?" she asks.

"Yeah," I reply. "It's like there's no passion between Angus and me. It's like we're going through the moves of love, but there's nothing below the surface. Especially - *and I'm only saying this because I'm tipsy* - especially in the bedroom. Do you know what I mean?"

Erin shrugs. "I don't, really."

"It's hard to explain. I just don't feel sexy at all. Sexy isn't *me*. It isn't *us*. Especially in bed. It's like we're robots or something just performing something lifeless and... dull."

Erin bites her lip, and her eyes glaze over. I know that face. She's thinking. There's a long pause. My heart beats in my chest rapidly as my best friend contemplates my words. It's so odd saying this stuff from deep inside me, but once I have it's like a dark cloud has been lifted and I feel light again.

"No problem's too big," Erin eventually says, a wide smile forming across her face. "Leave this to me. We'll get your sexy side out of you somehow."

\* \* \*

YEAH, I'm really bad with hangovers.

Even though the boozy lunch with Erin was yesterday, I'm still feeling the effects of it the next morning at work. It's like a repeat of that awful morning six months ago after the bachelorette party at the strip club when I was close to being sick in the trash can several times.

Yep. That bad.

And, just like that insane morning six months ago, here

I am back at the receptionist desk scrolling through my Instagram feed. Trying to put off the thudding ache running through my head.

I'm back on the profile of artists I admire. In the last six months, nothing has progressed with regard to my painting. I've not attended any classes, or barely have done any artwork at all. Dating Angus and work has taken up all my time.

But to be honest, it's also the *fear* of committing brush to canvas that's been the main thing stopping me.

I know I do have the time to devote to painting. I do have the talent. But every time I think of picking up a paint-brush, all those times I've been told *no* come back to haunt me and cause me to retreat. And I can't get those voices out of my head.

Then I hate myself for not even trying, and then the painful cycle starts again.

Another photo pops up on my phone. It's a painting by this up-and-coming teenager on the art scene. And it's *beautiful*. And she's younger than me.

*Oh god. I'm wasting my life sitting here when there are people like that doing amazing work.*

At the reception desk, I sigh and switch off my phone just in time to see Erin come skipping down the hallway towards me.

She's smiling.

*What does she have to smile so widely about at nine in the morning on a workday?*

"What is it?" I ask.

She comes to a quick stop in front of the desk. "Okay, here me out."

"Oh no, Erin. This already sounds like one of your crazy ideas."

"Hey, I don't have crazy ideas," she replies. "Well,

maybe one or two, but this isn't one of them. I can promise you."

I raise an unconvinced eyebrow. "If you say so."

"So, you know what we were talking about at lunch yesterday?"

"My memories of yesterday are *very* hazy, and I'm still recovering from it."

"You know, the whole thing with you and you-know-who?"

*Oh, I get it. My drunk admission of not feeling sexy?*

That whole thing? The thing I shouldn't have said out loud to my best friend?

Crap.

"Yeah?"

Inside, I'm cringing hard.

"Well, I've got a plan. Do you have anything on tonight?"

I pause and check my mental diary. "Nope."

"No? Perfect. I'm going to pick you up at seven."

"Oh, no. What is this, Erin?"

"Anna, I've got an ace up my sleeve."

# 9

YESTERDAY

*CHASE*

THE DRUNK GIRL's face is mere *inches* away from my crotch. I thrust my hips to bring my barely concealed cock even closer towards her face. She squeals excitedly.

I love it when they do that.

I slowly rock back and forth towards the girl like I'm fucking her nice and tenderly. I see her eyes go wild as she realizes that this is what a night with me looks like.

She wants me.

*But she can't have me.*

I twist around and travel back up the long stage of Club Xstasy to the steady beat of the Weeknd's *Earned It*. I move in rhythm to the song, feeling it pulsating deep within my core.

Oh, I can be such a pussy tease when I want to be.

I continue my erotic dance, the whole crowded room in

front of me screaming in orgasmic delight at my moves. The woman whose face just had my crotch in it a few moments ago seems to have fainted. I spot her collapsed in her seat, panting breathlessly and going cross-eyed. I smile triumphantly to myself.

*Yep, I've still got it.*

Dave the announcer appears behind me, a microphone in his hands.

"Beautiful ladies, give it up for Captain Chase!"

The room erupts in longing groans. The ladies clearly don't want me to leave.

*What a shame.*

Always leave your audience wanting more.

I spin off the stage as Dave warms up the audience for the next act with his smooth, deep voice. I head to my dressing room as more cheers echo down the backstage hallways.

The first thing I do once I get back in front of my mirror is to take a long swig of my water bottle.

Sweat pours off me. I reach for my towel and dry my face, flicking my light brown hair back.

*Another good night.*

I start to change my attire to something less revealing.

*And now it's time for a well-earned drink.*

Stacy slides me an opened bottle of beer the minute I plonk my sweaty ass down at Xstasy's bar. I shift myself around on the barstool to get myself comfortable before I gulp down the beer like it is water in a desert.

*I needed that.*

Stacy winks at me.

"You're a pro, Chase," she says as she flicks open another beer for me.

I flash her my trademark smile. "I'm just giving the ladies what they want."

"And what's that exactly?"

I don't miss a beat. "A good time."

Stacy rolls her eyes at me and then glides down the bar, finding the right ingredients for the next inevitable cocktail she'll have to make for the bachelorette party, drunkenly laughing at the other end of the counter.

I turn in my seat to face the stage, watching Ryan's Tarzan routine.

*He's still doing it?*

Yeah, it's getting real old.

I take another sip of my beer and lean back against the bar counter. I'm so preoccupied with critiquing Ryan's dreadful attempt at a Tarzan scream that I don't notice the woman slithering up next to me until it's too late.

"Hello handsome," she says.

I turn to look at her. I don't think I know her. She's not someone I instantly recognize. I hope she's not someone I've slept with and forgotten about. I don't want to be dealing with a confrontation so soon after a show. She has long, brown hair and brown eyes. Smooth skin. She's pretty.

And she doesn't seem angry at me. That's a good start.

"Hi," I reply to her. "Do I know you?"

I pray to God that she's not drunk. I can't have a moment now with some blacked-out bachelorette party girl who's clocked that I'm *that guy* from the stage.

"Oh, I seriously doubt that you know me, but I sure as hell know you," she replies.

"You know me?"

"Yep."

"Hm. Are you usually so cryptic?"

"Sometimes."

My ears prick up.

*Oh, I like this little interaction.*

"Are you going to tell me your name and what you're

doing talking to me, or are you going to stay mysteriously cryptic?" I ask.

"We'll see. I've got a proposition for you, Captain Chase."

"So, you know my name?"

"Of course."

"And what's this proposition, then?" I ask. I glance down at her cleavage. "What do you want me to do?"

She clocks onto my wandering eyes but doesn't point them out. "Oh, it's not for me," she replies slowly. "It's for my friend."

Now my ears are *really* pricking up.

"A threesome?" I ask.

She laughs. "Nothing like that. It's a bit more... unusual."

I really like where this is going.

"I'm listening."

"It's a strange request."

I chortle and take another sip of beer. "Honey, I work in a strip club. Trust me, I've heard it all."

*And I'll be down for anything, especially when there's the possibility of two women being involved.*

The mysterious girl narrows her eyes. "Okay, I'll be straight with you. I need you to give my friend private dance lessons."

*What?*

"Lessons? As in dance? As in *strip*?"

"Yes."

"Dancing?"

"Yes."

"You mean teach her to take her clothes off?"

"Well, you are a *stripper,* aren't you?"

"Yeah," I reply. "But I don't teach it."

"What do you mean? You do it every night up there."

She points to the stage.

*Does she not understand the difference?*

"Look, sweetheart, I'm not going to give your friend private dance lessons."

"Why not?"

"Because I just don't. My life is too busy, and besides, I'm no teacher."

"I can offer you payment, of course. Cash."

I get up off my stool to leave, taking my bottle of beer with me.

*Payment?*

Who does she think she is? She reckons she can just offer me some cash to do her bidding?

Does she think that I'll just accept some bills simply because I'm a male stripper strapped for dough?

"No way," I say, walking away. Shaking my head.

*Private dance lessons.*

Ha. What a joke.

I'm outta here.

But before I reach the end of the bar, she calls out to me.

"How about four thousand for seven weeks?"

I stop.

Is she saying what I think she's saying?

*That's a load of dough.*

I think of Brandi. The rent for the trailer. How far behind I am.

*You do need the money, Chase.*

"What's the catch?" I ask.

I'm not falling for no trap.

She shrugs. "Nothing, other than you having to give her a lesson for a couple of hours every week for the next seven weeks."

"One night every week for seven weeks?"

"Yep."

"That's it?"

She nods. "That's it."

I take a few steps back towards her.

*Fuck it. Let's see how much I can squeeze out of her.*

"I'll do it for eight thousand," I demand.

"Five."

"Six."

She smiles. "Deal."

*Ha.*

Rich girls.

*They don't know what a dollar means.*

She offers me her hand. I look down at it and reluctantly shake it.

What a crazy conversation this is turning out to be.

I hope I know what I'm getting into here. I know that this has the potential to backfire on my ass in a major way.

But money's money, right?

"Why me?" I ask her. "Why not simply pay some professional dance teacher in the city if you have so much cash to spend?"

"Because I've seen you in action," she replies, nodding at the stage. "I think you'll work."

"You've seen me dance?"

"These aren't just any private dance lessons," she says. "My friend needs her sexiness back. I'm hiring you to bring it out of her."

"Oh, don't worry. I can do that."

*Easy money.*

"Great."

I look around the club. "But we can't do it here," I say.

"It's fine," she replies. "I know a place."

"Okay."

She offers her hand out to me again. "Erin."

"Chase."

"Nice to meet you properly."

"So, when do you want me to start?"

* * *

I POKE my head around the door.

There's a whole load of young girls in the studio. Preteen. All lined up in a perfect row dressed in pink tutus stretching in front of mirrors.

Ballet dancers.

I quickly pull my head out and continue down the hallway.

*What the fuck am I doing here?*

I check the signs on the doors as I pass by them. Each one leads into a different dance studio.

There's a noticeboard with posters adorning it for ballet competitions.

*Yeah, really. What the fuck am I doing here?*

The money. That's it. I'm here purely for the money.

I would never be stepping into a fancy dance place like this if it wasn't for the money Erin's promised me.

*I hope she turns up. I hope this isn't some prank.*

I shake my head. I still can't believe what I'm doing. This whole thing better be real.

At the first sign of trouble, I'm going to walk straight out.

I check the sign for the next door.

*Studio eleven.*

That's mine.

I open the door and step inside.

It's a smaller room than the others I've passed. I have a quick look around. Bright lighting. Speakers. Everything I need.

I dump my bag in the corner and wander around the

room. A whole wall is just one big mirror. If what Erin says about her friend is true, then she's going to be *super* embarrassed seeing her reflection. Poor girl.

*What the fuck am I doing here?*

I feel like a performing monkey, pay in peanuts to make some chick happy.

But I need the money. I need to pay my rent.

I sigh and lean against the studio wall, my foot tapping anxiously.

*What the fuck am I really doing here?*

Seven weeks. That's how long I have to last.

I can do this.

I hear the squeak of the studio door opening.

I turn in anticipation. Must be Erin and her friend.

And then *she* walks in.

# 10

*ANNA*

"Erin, this is *definitely* one of your crazy ideas," I say when we walk into the reception of the dance studio. I look around me at the walls full of posters for ballet lessons and dance competitions with my mouth open.

I really can't believe she's dragged me along here tonight.

And I still don't know why she has. She's keeping that a big secret, much to my annoyance and her obvious satisfaction.

"Shut up and enjoy yourself," Erin giggles at me before turning to the receptionist. "Hi, I'm Erin. I've booked a studio."

The receptionist taps at a computer. "Studio eleven. It's upstairs."

"Thanks."

"Why are we even here, Erin?" I ask as my best friend pulls my arm, tugging me past the reception and up the stairs to the next level.

She told me to be ready at home for seven, but never told me *what for*. Even though I badgered her about it all throughout the day, she still didn't reveal her secret plan for tonight. Even when we pulled up outside the dance studio, I still didn't understand what was going on.

We're dancing?

*What does this entail?*

"Tell me why we're here," I demand, dragging my heels. "I'm not going up another step until you tell me."

Erin rolls her eyes. "Alright," she says, letting go of my arm. We stand in the middle of the staircase. I cross my arms, waiting for her explanation. "I'll say it."

*This better be good.*

"Go on."

"We're here to reclaim your sexiness."

"What?"

Erin smiles smugly. She's clearly proud of herself. "You were moaning about it so much the other day that I came up with this plan."

"I wasn't moaning."

She frowns at me. "You so were."

I raise an eyebrow. "Erin, what exactly are we doing here? You know I hate surprises."

"Exactly. It's fun."

"Not for me, this isn't."

"You want me to tell you straight?"

"Yes. Now."

Erin takes in a deep, self-satisfied breath.

"I've booked you seven weeks of dance lessons."

I nod. "Okay, dance lessons. Sounds cool. Not a big deal."

But Erin hasn't finished.

"With a male stripper."

My face drops.

*A male stripper? Dance lessons? Stripping?*

"You what?"

Erin continues to climb the staircase, ignoring my astonishment.

"Come on, Anna."

"Hang on, let me get this straight. You've booked me lessons to learn to dance *with a stripper*?"

"How many times do I have to repeat myself? Yes. Now, come on. We're going to be late."

"A *stripper*?"

"Yes."

"What the hell are you thinking?" I ask, bewildered.

I honestly can't believe this.

"He's the best I could think of, trust me."

"A stripper, though?"

"He will ignite a spark within you, I bet. Anna, you and your fiancé will be hanging off the chandelier in no time, having the most outrageous sex after a few lessons with this guy. Trust me."

"I don't trust you. This is insanity."

My best friend winks at me from the next level up. "We'll get that sexiness out of you. Come on."

I roll my eyes.

"This really is one of your crazy ideas."

"You know me."

I shrug and follow her up the stairs. "I don't even have any dance clothes," I say.

Erin lifts up the sports bag she's carrying. "Don't worry, I've thought of everything."

"God, you really have, haven't you?"

"Here's a spare change of clothes for you," she says. "They're mine, so don't rip them or there'll be hell to pay."

I shake my head and walk beside her until we reach studio eleven.

"I'm only doing this because I love you, Erin."

"After a few lessons with this guy, you'll be a slut in no time."

"I hope not."

"This must be the room," Erin says, opening the door to let me through.

I shoot her a look of exasperation as I step into the studio. She grins at me.

There's a man already in there.

*He must be the teacher-slash-stripper Erin's hired. I wonder how crazy he is. He must be if he's signed up willingly for this.*

I check him out.

And almost immediately, I recognize him. The big frame. The muscles. The aura of sex surrounding him.

*Holy shit.*

*Captain Chase?*

The guy from the strip club. The mad bachelorette party from six months ago. That dude?

The one I drunkenly fucked in the backstage of that club. That intense night I swore to myself to forget.

That guy?

He's standing there, in the studio Erin's booked.

Yep. It's definitely him. He's dressed differently this time than from what I remember, covered up much more than he was in a white t-shirt and tight jeans. But it's definitely him. I would recognize that chiseled jaw and green eyes anywhere.

*This is the guy who's going to be my teacher-slash-stripper?*

And he's looking at me as equally shocked as I must be looking at him.

I gulp.

Judging from his expression, he must recognize me as well.

This is insane.

His face changes into a wide smile as he sees me. "Hello," he says from across the room. Directed straight at me.

*He doesn't miss a beat, does he?*

I immediately turn and walk out of the room. Right past Erin.

I hear her telling him "one second," before she shuts the studio door and approaches me. I stand, shocked, in the middle of the hallway.

*No way it's him.*

But it's definitely the same dude from Xstasy, without a doubt.

What a nightmare I've walked into.

"What's wrong?" my best friend asks, sliding up to me.

She clearly doesn't understand the situation. She doesn't know the weird relationship between me and the stripper in that room.

"I can't do this," I reply. I'm not going to tell her the truth. I can't. I can't reveal what I once did with that man.

"Nonsense," Erin replies, frowning.

"I really can't."

"I've spent a lot of money on this dude," she says sternly.

"Erin, I can't do this."

"It'll be fine. He's from that strip club we saw six months ago. Remember that? Daria's bachelorette party? The army dude who gave you a good dance on the stage?"

"Oh, yeah," I reply through my teeth. "I remember. I remember him *crystal clear*."

"I thought he'll be a good idea."

"A good idea?"

"I've had to fork out a lot of money for this."

"I'm not doing it."

"Well, you're going in there whether you like it or not."

Before I know it, Erin's pushing me back into the room. Against my will. I stumble back in. Captain Chase stands there against the wall, smirking at the chaos erupting at the doorway.

*Glad to see someone's enjoying this.*

"Okay," I say to Erin. "Alright. I'm inside. Stop pushing me."

"Hello again," Chase says, taking a few steps towards me.

I eye him suspiciously, trying to give him telepathic clues to *not* talk about what happened six months ago in front of Erin. I really, really hope he doesn't.

"Hello."

"You're Erin's friend?" he asks.

He takes another step towards me. I keep my distance.

"Yep."

"The one I'm meant to be teaching dance to?"

"I guess so."

"The one who needs to relight her sexiness?"

I point a threatening finger at him. "Not like that," I reply.

He raises his hands. His gorgeous smirk still hangs on his face. "I'm only saying what she told me."

"Well, it's not like that."

*What has Erin organized for me? What has she got me into?*

"What's it like exactly?"

Erin steps into the room. "It's exactly like that," she says. "You're here to give Anna her mojo back."

"What? No." Both of them ignore me and my pitiful protestations.

"I need the money upfront," Chase says, turning to my best friend. "Cash."

"As long as you're here every Tuesday for the next seven weeks, then it's all good," Erin replies.

"Deal."

My best friend travels across the studio towards the hunk, pulling out a wad of bills. She quickly counts through them before handing them over to Chase.

I can't believe she's actually giving money to this guy.

"That's half the money there. The rest you'll get when the lessons are over," she says, ice cold.

Chase winks at her. "You're sly."

"Is that all good with you?"

"All good. You have my word. I'll be here for the next seven weeks."

"I don't think a stripper's word is worth much," I say under my breath, but they ignore me.

With the money handed over, Erin heads out the door. I hastily grab her arm before she leaves.

"Where are you going?" I ask her.

Erin laughs. "I'm not going to watch, Anna. This is for you to find your sexiness. It should be private."

"Stay. Please."

"I've got other stuff to do."

"Don't leave me." My plea is like a childish whimper.

My best friend laughs again. "You'll be fine. Have fun. Enjoy yourself. Find your sexiness."

And then she leaves, shutting the studio door behind her.

Leaving me alone with Captain Chase.

# 11

*ANNA*

"Just to let you know, before we do anything, I really, *really* don't want to be doing this," I tell Chase from across the dance studio. "Okay? For the record."

I cross my arms over my chest to doubly prove my unwillingness.

I can't believe Erin's left me alone in here. With *him*.

Chase smiles again at me for what seems like the hundredth time since I've stepped foot inside the dance studio, clearly happy with how uncomfortable I am. That smirk of his creeps across his face. That stupid, *sexy* smirk. "Alright, I've got it," he replies. "I'll note it down in the record."

He mimes writing an imaginary pen in the air. His green eyes light up as he does so.

*He thinks he's so funny.*

I do not.

"I was basically *forced* here," I explain. "I didn't even know what I was doing here until I was outside the room."

"Look, I'm not forcing you to do anything," the stripper replies, raising his hands. "You're a free woman, able to leave at any time you want to. Don't let me stop you."

"Trust me, you won't."

"But, for the record, since you're going on about it, I'll really like the rest of the money your friend has promised me," Chase continues. "I'll hate to lose it all just because you ain't willing to give this a go."

I shake my head in disgust. "Oh, I heard what you and Erin were talking about. It's all about the money for you."

"Your friend has paid for half the lessons. I'll like to see the other half if you don't mind."

"I do mind, and I honestly don't know why I'm still here."

"Why are you so upset?" Chase asks, walking towards me. "This is just some dance lessons."

I snort. "Dance lessons? You mean stripping?"

"It's dance."

"My friend is literally paying you to strip for me. I call that prostitution."

He chuckles. "This is definitely not prostitution, and it's going to even be barely stripping. I'm just going to teach you some basic dance moves, that's all."

I harrumph. "This is borderline sex."

"God, then you must've never have had good sex, then."

He realizes what he's said, what he's accidentally referred to, and his eyes go wide.

And that's my cue to smile.

*Ha.*

"Yeah, I've only ever had lousy sex."

It's not true, especially not in regard to Captain Chase, but I want to sting him where it hurts. His manliness.

He pauses, taking in a long, deep breath. "Okay. Let's address the elephant in the room."

I cross my arms even tighter against my chest. "I don't know what you're talking about," I reply.

"You do exactly. You're *her*. Six months ago? Club Xstasy? I know you recognize me."

*Great. So, he does remember that night.*

Ugh.

"Of course, I remember," I say. "But that was a long time ago."

Chase takes another step towards me. I stay rooted to the spot by the door.

"Six months. Not that long."

He's getting closer.

"And I was *drunk*. Really drunk."

Even closer.

"So was I."

He's right up in front of me now. Dwarfing me with his large, muscular frame. He towers above me, an absolute *hunk* of a man. I defiantly face up to him, my arms still crossed. I'm not going to let this man bully me around.

"It was all a mistake," I say. "A stupid careless mistake."

"Really? A mistake?"

"Yes."

Chase laughs. "It didn't *feel* like a mistake."

I want to strike at him, pound my fists against those delicious solid abs just inches away, but I know he's stating the truth.

*That night with him didn't feel like a mistake. Not at all.*

It was actually the complete opposite.

It was one of the most liberating and intense nights I've ever had.

And I've been dreaming about it – *touching* myself over it – for the last six months in a desperate attempt to relive those few hours of pure bliss.

I must be lost in my fantasy because Chase is staring at me, his piercing green eyes burrowing into my soul. He's waiting for my response. My silence says it all.

"Alright. It was... fun. But it wasn't me. It wasn't who I am."

"And who are you, exactly?"

I glare at him as if insulted by his question. "I'm a self-respecting woman. I don't do one-night stands, especially not with strippers."

And then there's that goddamn smirk again. "Oh, but you did, and I think you enjoyed it."

"That's enough."

Chase takes a step back. "Look, I'm happy for you to leave right now if you're uncomfortable with me. I can take the money your friend has given me right now and disappear. But Erin did tell me everything."

My eyes widen.

*What does he know?*

"She told you what?" I ask.

"You do want to feel sexier, don't you? You do want to actually *enjoy* being in bed with your fiancé?"

"She told you about my fiancé?"

*Okay, making a mental note to confront Erin with that little thing tomorrow.*

"She told me everything."

"Like what?"

"Well, you do *want* to ignite the relationship between you and your fiancé, don't you? You do want to unlock your inner sexual goddess?"

I stop.

He's right.

The bastard's right.

Erin knew *exactly* what she was doing when she set this all up. My best friend knows me so well. Maybe these dancing lessons are what I need, even if they are with *this* particular guy and even if my best friend did tell him everything.

I mean, if he was able to give me *that* night, then I'm sure he can make me get in touch with my sexier side.

And that's what I'm craving for right now.

*Think of Angus.*

I sigh.

"Alright."

Chase's eyebrows lift. "Alright?"

"I'll do these stupid classes."

"Good."

I'm sure he's thinking of the money. I bet he's hallucinating dollar bills falling from the sky right now.

"Let's just get one thing straight, okay?"

"Sure."

I point menacingly at him. "This whole thing. These dancing lessons. That's *all* they are. Okay?"

"Okay."

"No funny business. No seediness." I flash him my diamond engagement ring. "You see this here on my finger? I'm going to be a married woman soon, and the one thing I am not is a cheater. The *very* last thing. You got that?"

Chase's smile disappears. "I understand."

Good. It seems like he takes this as seriously as I do.

"Let's put the past behind us, okay?" I ask.

"I've already forgotten about that night," Chase replies. "Trust me, I'm not going to try anything, especially when there's money on the line. I need it more than my dick needs pussy."

"*And* you can stop being rude."

He throws his hands up. "Hey, that's just how I talk."

"Well, I don't like it."

"Fine. Mature language censored, then. I got it."

"Okay," I exhale. "This might work for the both of us. You get your money and hopefully, you uphold the end of your side of the bargain and you actually teach me a thing or two."

Chase raises his hand. "Deal."

I shake it.

"Deal."

He nods at Erin's sports bag by the front door. "You should get changed now."

I gasp. "Not in front of you."

*Is he already trying to be naughty? Straight after that serious conversation? He wants to see my naked body?*

I'm prepared to walk out here right now.

Chase laughs and points to the other end of the dance studio. "No, not in front of me. In the bathroom. It's through there."

I spot the doors.

"Oh. Of course."

Chase shakes his head and turns to the sound system, plugging in his phone.

*Well. That was embarrassing.*

Two minutes in and I've already fucked it.

Gingerly, I pick up the sports bag and sprint into the bathroom. I blush the entire way across the room. Chase keeps his back to me, playing with his music selection.

*You're such an idiot, Anna.*

I dress in the clothes Erin's packed for me. Yep, they're much easier to dance in. More sporty than my usual attire. Then I step back into the studio. Chase is stretching, thudding club music blaring from the speakers.

He turns to me.

"So this is just about taking your clothes off, right?" I ask as I nervously walk up to the stripper.

He frowns. "Oh no. It's more than that, Anna. This is

dancing in its *purest* sense. It's a professionally choreo-graphed routine. It isn't just *taking your clothes off*. This takes skill."

"Skill?"

"Care and attention. It's making love on stage. It's revealing yourself to the audience. There might be gimmicks like the costumes and the music and the scenarios, but what I'm doing up there on stage is showing the truth."

"Which is?"

"That everyone fucks. Everyone makes love. Everyone wants to feel that primal urge take over, even if it's just for a few moments. That no matter who we are or where we're from, all humans want to sweat and feel another person touch them in places they barely dare to touch themselves."

"Do you practice that speech in the mirror?" I ask.

"Every morning when I wake up," Chase replies with his trademark smirk.

"You have an answer for everything, don't you?"

"Well, before we can start properly. Tell me about your-self, Anna."

"You know about me."

"I want to hear you describe yourself."

"What do you want to know?"

"Your life. Right now."

*What can I say?*

"Um, well, I'm getting married, as you know."

God, this is so embarrassing.

"Not just that. How do you feel about it?"

I'm cringing up inside.

"I don't really know how I feel. I mean, I'm happy about getting married and all, but it's all so sudden. There are a lot of things I want to do before settling down."

Chase nods. "You want to experience some freedom. You've been denied some wild years."

"If you know anything about me, then you'll know *wild* is the exact opposite of who I am."

"How so?"

"I'm not *wild*, Chase."

"I can point out a night six months ago that'll say the opposite."

I glare at him. "I thought we promised not to talk about that night."

"Sure. There must be more to it all, though."

*Is this man pretending to be a qualified therapist?*

"Um, I guess a lot of things boil down to my dad. He's a very... controlling man. He actually put Angus and me together."

Chase's eyebrow raises inquisitively. "Is that so?"

"He'd kill me if he found out I was here taking private dance classes."

"Your dad or your fiancé?"

I laugh nervously. "Both."

"Well," Chase says. "Let's make sure we make it worthwhile, then."

There's a long pause. He's actually a really easy person to talk to. Who'd knew a male stripper would actually be so good at listening?

Maybe I should be here. Maybe these lessons will really help me.

"I just want to feel sexy again," I whisper.

"Well," Chase replies with his smile. "I'm here to help that."

# 12

*ANNA*

ANGUS TURNS to me when we pull up outside my parents' place. He turns off the ignition, twirling his keys around his finger while he continues to stare at me.

"What is it?" I ask, nervous.

His long glare is making me uncomfortable.

His reply is brisk and stern.

"Erin's told me what you're doing."

I blink.

"What do you mean?"

"These dance lessons." His words drip with disgust. "She's told me what you're doing."

*Oh no.*

"Yeah, she's paid for some," I reply. "She thinks it'll be good for me to do them. Get my body moving, you know?"

*How much has she really told him?*

Angus flicks his attention away from me to my parent's house. His hands tap absent-mindedly on the steering wheel, thinking. "Right."

"It's just some fun. Erin thought it'll be something silly for me to do before the wedding. I've always wanted to learn how to dance properly anyway, so what better time than now?"

"Hm."

Angus is being silent.

I don't like it when he's silent.

"Don't tell Mom or Dad," I whisper. "They don't really... understand these types of things."

Angus doesn't reply. Instead, he unlocks the door and steps out into the evening air.

*Is he upset with me for taking up private lessons?*

He doesn't give me time to ask him why. He's already at the house, ringing the doorbell of my parent's place.

I quickly scurry out of the car, following him anxiously.

To be honest, my parents don't live in a house, they live in a *mansion*. And this is the mini palace where I grew up. I always found it weird, growing up in a building this size for only three people. There are more rooms in there than a small hotel. We could host an entire army inside these four walls. I always felt lonely growing up in here with no brother and sister to play with. Sometimes I wouldn't even see one of my parents for a full day when they were in another part of the house; it was just that big.

The place looks like what a stereotypical mansion should look like. All white pillars and long windows. An immaculate garden kept by a small workforce of cleaners and grounds people. Like a slice of Regency England placed down awkwardly in the middle of an American city.

My parents answer the door, and we exchange the usual formalities. I'm used to this world of decadence and power, but even then I still find it strange. Angus clearly does not. He fits in with my parents' mansion like the furniture. No wonder Dad seems to love him so much; he's basically speaking to a younger version of himself.

*Yep. Angus really is the perfect match for a woman like me.*

After our greetings and handshaking, we all sit down around the lavish dinner table. My parents have hired a chef for the evening, just for Angus and me. He brings out a whole three-course meal prepared in the restaurant-quality kitchen in the house.

We sit, eat, and drink. Fine vintage wine and real silver cutlery. I don't speak much. Angus and Dad are dominating the space, as all men of the Jensen family are want to do.

*Angus really is going to fit in well with my family.*

Mom and I sit silent, slowly eating dinner. Mom is comfortable being a quiet, obedient wife. She's had decades of practice.

This is my life. My future. This was where and how I was raised.

It is nearly the end of the meal when Angus first raises the topic I really don't want him to do.

"Anna is taking dance lessons," he says. Out loud. To everyone.

The dinner table falls silent for a moment as my parents take in what he's just revealed.

I shoot a glare full of daggers at Angus, but he ignores me. He doesn't even look at me. He's too busy trying to sidle up to Dad.

*I specifically asked him not to say that.*

My fiancé is enjoying riling me up, and I can't say anything in front of my parents. He knows that.

"Dance lessons?" Mom asks.

There's a ding as Dad places his cutlery on his plate. "What kind of dancing?" he asks.

All eyes turn to me.

I shrug. "Just a load of different types," I lie. "A whole range of dancing. It's a bit of fun."

Dad chuckles and leans towards Angus as if he's telling him a joke. "Fun? Sounds like a frivolous waste of time. *Dancing*."

"I agree," my fiancé replies, smiling at me. "I don't see the point in it."

*I can't believe what's going on here.*

"It's just some fun," I retort softly.

"That kind of *fun* is for girls, not adults like us," Dad says, and I'm experienced enough to sense another one of his lectures coming on. "We *don't* dance, Anna. You know that. People like us are respectable members of society. Board members. Corporate businesspeople. We don't take up frivolous side activities like schoolchildren after school. Leave the dancing to people who can throw their lives away on such wasteful enterprises."

"It's just a class once a week."

"Nothing is every just a class," Dad replies. "What will others think when they find out about this? Our friends?"

"I like it," I say, but my voice is no louder than a whisper. I look to Angus to help me, for my fiancé to step in and defend me, or at the very least change the subject. He doesn't do anything but nod his head in agreement with Dad.

"It's also just *embarrassing*," Dad continues. He's on a roll now. He can't be stopped. "Dancing. Doing it in public, wearing the kind of things you need to wear to do that. It's too *revealing*. Too *common*. What was that thing you were really obsessed about when you were younger, Anna?"

It takes me a moment to understand what he means.

*Oh.*

I don't want to admit it out loud because I know what

he'll say next, but Mom and Angus are staring at me. I'm under pressure. I just want this torture to end.

"Painting?"

"That's it," Dad exclaims. "Your *painting*. See, it's like dancing. Frivolous pastimes. They should be left to teenage girls. You grow out of those phases in life when you become a respectable adult."

"I agree, Mr. Jensen," Angus says. "Frivolous."

I can't believe he's betraying me like that. I've mentioned to him a few times how passionately I feel about artwork, and about how much I want to dip my toe into those waters again. And yet after all that, he just rats me out at the first chance he gets to slime his way up to Dad.

"And what about art?" I ask. I need to say something. I can't have the only things I care about ripped apart like this.

Dad squints. "What about it?"

"What would you say to professional artists who do painting for a living? You have artwork hanging all over this house. What do you say to the people who painted them?" I point out.

Dad shakes his head patronizingly, like I'm just his little baby girl again asking him about fairies. "That world is not for us, Anna. Not for you. We're above that. Would you prefer to live poor and *paint*, or to live the lives we live and actually *do* something?"

Angus laughs.

I stare down at my plate. There's nothing I can say to that. I know there's nothing I can do to change my dad's mind.

I feel so alone.

I place my knife and fork together. "Excuse me," I say to no one in particular. "I need to go to the washroom."

I leave the dining table, glancing over at Angus to see him take a sip of his wine. Acting like nothing had happened. He knows me, though. He must know how much pain I'm in by my father's words.

I hold in my breath and exit the room. I refuse to breathe until I head all the way up the grand marble staircase to the next level.

I don't go to the bathroom. I instead take a left upstairs and enter my old bedroom.

It's only then that I allow myself to breathe again.

I softly close the door shut behind me and turn on the light. My old bedroom comes to life right before my eyes. Even though I only come back to this house for a dinner party every few weeks, it's been a long time since I was last in this room. It's still laid out like it was when I was a teenager last living here. All my soft toys lie on the pink bed. Old photos of high school are stuck to the wall. I take a moment to scan my eyes around the room, taking in all the memories, until I spot a box in the corner.

I know what's in it.

I haven't opened it in years.

I take in another deep breath and cross the room towards it. Now's the best time to open it again after all this time.

And I do.

I pull out the contents. Old paintings of mine. The first ones I ever did when I was a teenager. Little canvases of my first ever attempts at putting brush to color. They're all there. I ruffle through the collection, smiling warmly at myself.

Nothing has ever made me happier than when I painted these. I still vividly remember the feel, the touch, the smell of paints, and the colorful mess I made as I let out my soul on the canvas.

And then the decision comes to me.

*I'm going to keep these.*

I'm going to take them home. Screw Dad and what he was saying at the dinner table; I really do love painting. I'm not too old for it.

I reach into the cupboard and pull out an old backpack. I carefully hide the canvases in there and zip it up securely.

*Now to get them to the car.*

You know what? Fuck it. I will.

I sneak out of the room and quietly head down the stairs, careful not to alert anyone else to my antics. I slide out the front door and head across the path to the car. I shove the bag into the back, where I know Angus won't check. I fix my hair in the mirror and turn back towards the house.

"What are you doing out here?"

It's Angus. He's standing by the front door, staring at me.

*I hope he hasn't noticed what I've just done.*

"I needed some fresh air," I reply. I'm not a good liar.

He continues staring at me for a while before he speaks again. "I don't believe you," he says.

"What do you mean?"

He chuckles. "Only joking."

"Oh."

"You can look so guilty sometimes, Anna. It's cute."

"Stop it."

"You know that if you are hiding anything from me, I will find out."

I stop.

"Yeah, I do," I reply softly.

"Come on," he says. "Let's go back inside."

* * *

I LEAN against the car window and watch the lights of the city flash by. Angus sits quietly next to me, no music playing, as we make our way back to his apartment.

*Angus' apartment.*

It's actually my new home, but I'm still not used to it.

I sigh and turn in my seat, sneaking a quick glance at the dark backpack below the back seat. Angus hasn't spotted it yet, and I hope he doesn't.

I don't even know why I took those early paintings of mine with me. I just wanted to. It was a completely spontaneous act. So unlike me.

But I'm happy I did.

"Do you really think what you said back there at my parents' house?" I ask Angus as he turns a corner.

"Think what?"

"That paintings are frivolous like Dad said. Do you really think so?"

Angus scrunches up his face like I'm suddenly speaking a foreign language. "It is frivolous though, Anna."

"But were you just saying that to please Dad?"

"No."

"Okay."

I don't believe him.

"Why?" he asks.

I lean back against the window. "Nothing," I reply. "It doesn't matter."

# 13

*CHASE*

I THROW on my tight-fitting leather jacket and open my trailer door. Flicking my keys out of my pocket, I make my way across the yard towards my parked motorcycle. I always feel a pang of pride when I see her. She's a beautiful machine, sleek and fast. Women love to ride on the back of her, their arms eagerly wrapped around my waist as we shoot down the highway. My motorcycle is better at getting me pussy than an actual human wingman.

The evening air is crisp as I jump onto the back of my bike. I feel the leather of the seat against my crotch as I swing my leg over it. I'm so used to riding her now that the motorcycle is like an extension of my body. I first learned to ride one when I was barely sixteen, soon after I left home to make my own way in the world. An older stripper taught me how to ride. He also taught me how to dance.

Ever since that day, my motorcycle has represented my freedom to me. My ability to do anything and go wherever I want.

I'm about to turn on the ignition when I'm furiously tapped on the shoulder from behind.

I shift around on my bike.

*Oh great.*

It's Brandi, and she doesn't look happy.

*Here we go.*

"Where's my money?" she demands aggressively, thrusting her hand in my face.

I smile, ignoring her pent-up energy. "Brandi. I was just coming to see you."

"Bullshit," she replies, spit oozing from her mouth. "Where's the rent?"

"That was what I was going to see you about," I say, reaching into my jacket's inside pocket. The trailer park manager's eyes widen. She probably thinks I'm about to pull out a gun or something. I'm not that crude.

She takes a step back as I pull out my hand. I'm holding a wad of bills. The money Erin had given me last week at the dance studio. I offer it to her.

"There you go."

"What is this?"

"It's called currency, Brandi. You can buy goods and services with it."

She ignores my joke.

"How much is this?"

"That should cover most of my back payments. I'll have the rest for you in a couple of weeks."

She flicks through the bills, dollar signs practically flashing in her eyes. I'm glad she's pleased.

"Where did you get this from?" she asks.

I give her a look.

"Do you even care, Brandi? Don't ask a man like me a question like that."

She harrumphs and twirls away, back down the road to her trailer park office.

Well, I'm glad she's happy. Erin's money has probably saved me from getting jumped on by Brandi's gangster cousins. It's brought me a couple of weeks, and then I'll have the rest of the dance money and then I'll be all good.

I shake my head as I watch Brandi disappear.

*These lessons better pay off.*

I start my motorcycle and zoom on out of there.

* * *

BECAUSE OF MY interaction with Brandi, I'm late for the dance lesson. I'm made even more aware of how late I actually am when I spot Anna standing outside the studio as I pull up on my bike.

And she, like Brandi, doesn't look pleased.

*What is it with women today? Is the moon in the wrong position or something?*

She glares at me as I park the motorcycle, her foot tapping and her arms crossed. As usual.

"You're late," she says sternly.

"I am."

"Is that all you're gonna say?"

"Yep."

"And *why* are you late?"

I shrug. "I just am. Shall we go inside?"

"Not until you apologize."

"Apologize for what?"

"For being late."

I shake my head.

"Well, you're wasting time now. Let's get started."

I brush past her into the building. She grunts and follows me.

The first lesson we had together last week was *interesting*, to say the least. I was ready to walk out of there the minute she opened her mouth and started to berate me, but she did have me curious. It was weird she was angry at me for the night we shared. I don't know why she would be when it seemed like she enjoyed it so much. But I enjoyed riling her up in our lesson together. It was kinda fun. She's sassy. I like that.

I was close to just walking out in our first lesson, but then I decided maybe the money and the company of Anna might be fun after all.

Learning about her shitty fiancé and her controlling father was just the icing of the cake. It made me even more curious to find out more about her.

She skips up the stairs beside me, still accosting me for being late all the way to our studio.

"You know how rude it is to keep someone waiting? We said seven, and you turn up nearly half an hour later. I can't believe I actually *waited* for you."

I ignore her. Instead, I check her out. I didn't get a good look at her during the last lesson in between our bickering and banter. But now, as she walks beside me, I've got a much better view of her.

She's even prettier than when I remember her back in my dressing room. Silky skin. Dark blonde hair. Grey eyes. I remember her touch six months ago. The way she responded to my own touch. How she gasped when I penetrated deep inside her. Her eyes that went wild. How much she whispered, begging me to get inside her. Oh, I remember it all. My cock twitches at the memory. She was an immeasurably good fuck.

She does a thing with her lips where she slightly bites them when she's angry. She's doing that a lot as she pesters me about my lateness. I think it's very cute. Makes me want to kiss her.

But I know I can't. Like her, I also take cheating seriously. She told me her boundaries, and I'm going to respect them.

*Remember, Chase. You're not here for a good fuck, you're here for the money.*

That's all.

I open the door to the dance studio. Anna is still going on about how *rude* I am. How *inconsiderate* I've been. *La la la.*

"I'm sorry," I say.

That stops her barrage. She blinks at me, clearly not expecting me to apologize.

"You're sorry?"

"I am. I had something urgent I needed to do. I'm sorry for holding you up."

She flicks her hair back. "Oh, okay. That's all you needed to say." She's hesitant.

I know what she thinks of me. I see it in her eyes. She probably thinks of me as some kind of monster. Some dumb stripper. Some hot dude who sits around doing nothing but fuck girls and drink beer. Some lazy guy who thinks of nothing but himself, and she's not far from the truth. But there's more to me than meets the eye.

Maybe I'm not only that dumb stripper playboy, and maybe I can show her that.

"Let's start," I say, ushering her into the studio.

"What do you want me to do?" Anna asks, folding her arms.

This is going to be a lot harder than I thought.

*I should just walk out of here right now.*

"First, I'm going to teach you to dance rough and dirty."

Anna raises an irritated eyebrow. "Rough and dirty?"

"Yep."

"No way are you making me do something like that."

I smile. "How about you give it a try first and then you can decide whether or not you like it?"

"I don't like the term *rough and dirty*."

"Relax, it's just the way we're gonna dance."

She rolls her eyes. "No funny business."

"No funny business."

"Alright."

We start the lesson.

I've been teaching her basic moves. Stuff you'd find any decent dancer performing on the dance floor at a nightclub. Moves to attract the opposite sex, moves to flaunt your body. Most of the problems with amateur and new strippers is just getting them to discover how their own bodies move. To make them feel confident in their skin. Confident in their sexuality.

"Confidence is key," I tell Anna as I wrap my hands around her, showing her exactly where to place her own.

Our bodies touch. I feel her ass push into my groin.

But we're keeping this formal.

*No funny business.*

"How do I become more confident?" she asks.

Even though we're up close and personal, everything is strictly business. I know she's getting married soon, and I'm not going to mix the money I've been promised with my base instincts trying to fuck her. But it's hard to ignore that side of myself.

I just remain focused on the moves.

I'm here to teach. Not seduce.

"Move your body," I reply to Anna. "This is a safe space for you to make mistakes. Just explore how your body moves, what turns you on. What makes you open up. Listen to the beat of the music, that's your guide. Stick to it and you can't go wrong."

I begin to show her some moves of my own. Moves that are so basic anyone can perform them, but ones I still use today. Sometimes the simplest things can cause the most intense reaction in my audience.

She's definitely better than last week. I've never really taught dance before, and it's a high to see how much she's improved in a week.

I'm actually kinda proud.

"Let's start with the hips," I say, sidling up to her. I place my hands around her waist, guiding her body to the music. "Just in and out, in and out. You're in control. You want to make him want you. You want to show him that you're in control, that you know what you want. Like I said, confidence is key."

We keep at it for the next hour. The time flies past.

*Are you actually enjoying this, Chase?*

You know what? I actually am.

Wow.

Didn't expect that a week ago.

But then the lesson comes to an end. The time runs out.

"Thank you," Anna says. "That was... good."

"Yeah, I think so too," I reply.

She smiles at me. I think this is the first time she has done that since that night six months ago. Maybe I am proving to her I'm more than some horny stripper.

She heads off into the bathroom to get changed. I unplug my phone from the speaker system, leaning over her bag to do so.

Her bag is open. By chance, I accidentally peek inside. Something bright catches my eye. Something unusual.

I know it's not right to look inside someone's bag, but I

couldn't help it leaning over like that. There is something in there. Green and blue.

Without thinking, I pull it out.

It's a canvas. A painting. Bright colors. Abstract, but definitely some kind of landscape. It's beautiful.

"What are you doing?"

Anna's emerged from the bathroom. She stares at me. Shocked.

"Did you paint this?" I ask.

"What are you doing?" she repeats.

"I'm no artist, but it looks amazing."

"Are you snooping around my bag?"

"It was open, and I saw this. It's really impressive, Anna."

"Were you snooping around for my money? Is that what you want?"

I shake my head in disbelief. "No, that's not true."

*How can she think that?*

"How dare you."

She storms over, snatching the canvas from my hands. She grabs her bag from between my feet and heads out the door.

She's gone before I can say anything. Before I have the chance to defend myself from her wild accusation.

Shit.

*You've really fucked up this time, Chase.*

# 14

*ANNA*

"I've got a delivery for a Mr. Dunn."

I look up from the reception desk at the man standing in front of me gripping a large cardboard package.

"Great," I reply. He offers me a touchpad to sign for the delivery. I then take the package from him. It's heavier than I thought. It bangs hard against the counter as it nearly slips through my hands.

This is who I am. A human collector for deliveries.

The man nods at me and jumps back into the elevator.

I fall back into my receptionist chair and sigh.

I only got this job because of Dad. My whole life was planned for me since birth, all the way down to meticulous detail. Dad didn't want me to go to college and choose my own way in life, instead straight after I graduated high school, he put me in the job as a receptionist at his company until the time someone would come along and marry me. And that's exactly what happened with Angus.

I guess Dad's plan for me is working out perfectly. He's

going to marry off his daughter and get the son he always wanted.

I swivel around in my chair.

Maybe I'm so grumpy this morning because of last night. I'm still angry at what happened. Seeing Chase just rummaging through my bag like that, *pulling* out that painting I made when I was a teenager. It was wrong of him. So wrong.

*Why did he think he had the right to go through my stuff?*

I don't want to see him again. He'd crossed a line when he did that.

He did say my painting was amazing, though. Why was he looking at it? Why would he say that?

No one has ever said my paintings were good before. Chase had given me my first compliment for my art, and I hate him for it.

I don't want to think of him again.

*DING.*

The elevator doors open.

I glance up from the desk.

My mouth drops open.

It's Chase.

*What.*

He's appeared as if by magic, as if me thinking about him has somehow willed him into existence. As if he's deliberately here because I've cursed him in my head.

He casually strolls out of the elevator as if him being here is normal.

And I can't believe it.

The stripper is standing in *my* workplace.

He spots me straightaway. How could he not when I'm sitting right there in front of him?

"Hello, Anna." It's like he's suppressing a laugh when he says my name.

*What is it with his permanent smug confidence?*

I turn my head, making sure no one else is within earshot.

"What the *fuck* are you doing here, Chase?"

"I thought I'll come and see you." He whistles as he glances around the office. "Boy, you really are high up here. This is your family's company?"

"Seriously, Chase," I say urgently under my breath. "What are you doing here? Get out."

"I've come to give you this," he approaches the desk.

At least he's clothed in his white shirt and trademark leather jacket.

I sink back into my chair, dismayed by his cocky demeanor. He's acting like he owns the place.

"What is it?" I ask.

Chase lifts his hands up and places something large and square on top of the reception counter. "A present," he replies. "For you."

I glare at him. "What the hell do you think you're doing here, and with this? Whatever it is. Leave, Chase."

"I got this for you, Anna. As a sort of... apology for last night."

"I don't need your apology or some random gift. We're through, Chase. You looked through my stuff and that's a big *no no*."

"I honestly didn't mean to go through your shit. I just saw the painting, and I picked it out."

"I don't care. The dance lessons are over," I whisper in reply, my voice growling. "I don't even know why I signed up to them in the first place."

"Just take the present, Anna."

"No."

"Yes."

"No."

"What are you, a child?" he asks sarcastically. "Just take the damn present."

I glower at him, but I still take the wrapped-up square off the counter and fit it under my desk. Reluctantly. I make sure it's out of sight from any wandering eyes. I don't need my work colleagues to ask me where I've got it from.

"Happy now?" I ask the stripper.

He smiles.

"All happy."

"So, can you leave now?"

"Nope."

"Why not?"

"I need to ask you a question," he says.

"Don't play games with me, Chase. I took your silly present. Now just leave."

"Are you going to be at the dance lesson next week?"

Before I can answer, a hand clasps onto Chase's shoulder from behind.

"How's everything here, Anna?"

It's Angus.

He's somehow silently approached us.

I look at my fiancé standing behind the stripper.

*The two men. Together.*

I really can't believe what I'm seeing.

"This is my dance teacher, Chase," I say slowly to Angus. "Chase, this is my fiancé, Angus."

My fiancé scans the stripper up and down, taking him all in. He doesn't seem impressed, but he still offers out his hand.

And Chase shakes it.

And there's a brief awkward silence.

There's so much tension in this room.

Two men squaring up to each other. And they clearly don't like each other one *inch*.

"Hi, Chase. Anna's told me about your lessons," Angus growls.

"Oh, has she?" Chase raises his eyebrow at me. "Is that all she's told you about me?"

"What else is there for me to know?" Angus asks.

Chase shrugs. "Not much, I guess."

"You don't think highly of yourself?"

"I didn't say that," Chase replies.

*Oh God, is there going to be a punch up right here in front of me? One level down from Dad's office?*

I mean, despite my horror, the thought of two men actually physically fighting over me is kinda hot.

"Good," Angus replies.

There's another awkward pause.

"Chase was just leaving," I say, trying to diffuse the situation.

The stripper turns to me. "Was I?"

"Yes." I'm firm.

I want this whole thing to end as quickly as it started. I'm so aware of Chase's present tucked in next to my foot. I hate how I have to sit here whilst Angus and Chase face up to each other like they're in some kind of gladiator match.

"Well, then. Bye."

Chase gives me a quick salute, then he's back in the elevator.

And, to my horror, Angus follows him inside.

# 15

*CHASE*

"I'll travel down with you," Angus says as he presses the elevator's *closing doors* button.

"It's no need," I reply.

But it's too late.

The elevator doors are already shutting. Before they close fully, I glimpse Anna staring at both Angus and me, her mouth open.

She's shocked at what's happening, and I don't blame her.

*Yep. Me too.*

The elevator descends the many levels of the skyscraper. Both Angus and I are silent for a moment inside the small metal room as we feel ourselves fall.

There's not a lot of space in here if we come to blows.

*If.*

I eye up Anna's fiancé. He's shorter than me by a considerable amount. He's handsome, I guess. In that kind of rich douchebag way. Expensive suit. Expensive watch.

*Just Anna's type.*

Exactly what I imagined when she described him to me.

Angus and I are *very* different men.

He breaks the silence by turning around to face me, his lips curled in a sneer.

"Are you planning to fuck her?" he asks quietly. Menacingly.

I laugh. "Are you being serious?"

*He's going with this straight out the gate?*

"I am. Are you planning to fuck my future wife?"

I don't need his words to understand how serious he is; Angus' stern face does all the talking.

*Is the man insane?*

"Trust me, Angus," I say. "Anna is the last woman I'd be after."

*If only he knew what happened six months ago.*

Anna was good. Real good back then.

That was before she met douchebag mcdoucheface over here.

"Hm."

Angus doesn't sound convinced by my answer. He turns away from me, towards the door.

*I don't even know why I'm giving this rude bastard the time of day.*

"I think I get enough girls without needing yours, Angus. I don't like being used by women with a ring on their finger."

I'm smirking. I know I'm being bad, that I'm deliberately teasing him, but it's just too much *fun*. If he's going to try to intimidate me by riding the elevator down with me, then I've got every right to rile him up like this.

"Right."

"Although I would be pretty intimidated too if my girlfriend was taking private dance lessons from an incredibly sexy tutor," I continue.

*Oh, I'm really pushing the line here.*

Angus's hands twitch. They're slowly squeezing into fists.

I'm watching him carefully. I've learned from past experiences that there's nothing crazier than some rich businessman, high on power, swinging a wild emotional punch at you. With their pampered lifestyles, they don't even know how to fight half the time, but that makes them even more reckless and unpredictable.

And I can't afford a punch to my face. Besides my crotch, that's my main money maker on stage.

"You're a joker, aren't you?" he asks me flatly. "A real joker who thinks he's hilarious."

I flash him my trademark smirk. "I like to give people a good time."

"Yeah. A good time. I don't know the antics you get up to on stage, but they're not welcome around my future wife. You got that?"

"I got it crystal clear, mate. Trust me, Angus. I wouldn't touch her like that with a ten-yard medieval lance."

"Don't think I don't know what you're up to, Chase," Angus warns.

It's a pretty pathetic attempt at scaring me. Maybe this guy should take some pointers from Brandi.

"And what am I up to, *Angus*?"

"You've got a lot of balls coming here today," he replies. "Coming to her work."

"I do have a lot of balls, Angus. Thank you. But the reason for my little trip was only to organize our next dance lesson."

"And you couldn't do that via text?"

"Technology and I don't get along. I prefer talking in person."

"You're a real smartass, you know that?"

"I try to be."

*Oh, he's real threatened by me, isn't he? I like this.*

The elevator doors *ding* open, revealing the lobby of the skyscraper. I bow dramatically to Angus, letting him out first. I follow him towards the large spinning glass doors leading outside.

"Don't think that because you're so cocky, Chase, that you can run off with my girl."

"I hate cheaters, Angus. More than any man I know."

It's the god-honest truth.

"Because I'm different from other men, Chase," Angus says. "I've got money. Prestige in this town. And I'm not afraid to use my power."

"Real scary stuff. I'll keep it in mind."

"Don't you even think of touching her."

"Don't worry, Angus, you have nothing to worry about from me," I say to him. "Cheating really isn't my game. I'm just doing this for the money."

We both come to a stop before the front doors.

"Good," Angus replies. "Because she's above you."

*The bastard.*

"Above me?"

His eyes scan me up and down in disgust. "You're just some stripper, and she's a *Jensen*. And soon she's going to be an Allen, and you're nothing but some poor stripper."

As tempting as it is to tell this smug bastard that I actually had sex with his fiancée before he met her, I can't do that to Anna. I'm not that much of a shit, however satisfying it would be to smear that information into this dick's face.

"Well, she may soon be an *Allen*, but she's still taking dance lessons with me," I reply.

The truth is a bit too much for dear old Angus. I see the tension build up in him, his vein close to popping on the side of his sunbed-tanned neck.

"I'm watching you closely, *Captain Chase*. Don't think I don't know everything about you, that I don't have the resources to follow you if I want."

*What kind of bastard am I dealing with here?*

"Are you threatening me?" I ask.

"Of course not," he replies, smiling. "I just want you to know the full consequences if you do try anything."

Before I could reply, the man pulls out a hundred-dollar bill and slides it into my pocket.

*Money?*

I can't believe it. The sheer insult.

"Just because I might not have a load of daddy's cash in my bank account doesn't mean I want your money," I say as I pull out the bill and throw it back into Angus' face. He blinks but doesn't even bend over to pick the bill up.

"How much would it cost to make you disappear?" he asks under his breath. "I bet you're cheap, considering you're nothing but a stripper."

"Do you usually interfere with your fiance's wishes like that? I'll keep teaching her to dance until she says stop."

"Oh, really?"

He's really got me going now.

"Maybe if you were better in bed, then she wouldn't need to come to me for dance lessons," I reply.

The man's face drops. His cheeks flare red.

He's ready for it.

"You want me to beat you up?" he asks.

Yep. *Pathetic.*

"I bet you've never thrown a fist in your life," I reply.

I watch Angus' nose twitch. His body's rigid.

*Yeah, he's never been in a fight.*

"You want to bet on it? With what money?"

He tries staring me down. It doesn't really work when I am a whole load of inches taller than him and have about his body weight in muscle mass.

He's a stubborn bastard, I'll give him that. He doesn't know when to stop.

I lean over him and whisper. "I bet my entire life savings one punch from me will knock you out cold for days. How would that look in front of your fiancé, in front of your workplace? In front of her dad?"

I'm so close to him that I see the hesitation in his eyes. He shuffles back a step. He's trembling.

*Serves him right for trying to play with the big boys.*

"Don't ever threaten me again," I say.

Angus's head turns to a group of security guards standing by the front doors. I see he's about to call out to them for help.

*Ah. So, he is a coward.*

"Don't worry, I'm leaving," I say, raising my hands.

I head out the front doors of the skyscraper. I turn around before I leave, unable to resist one final look. Angus is still standing there where I left him. I bet he's shaking in terror.

"Don't worry, I would never touch her when she has a little asshole fiance," I call out.

I'm not one to casually throw around my size, but when dicks like Angus try to threaten me like that, I have no choice.

I might be a big guy, but I know Angus was right when he said he had the resources to track me. I may be able to intimidate him in a simple fistfight, but he has the money to make my life hell.

I've just got to keep a low profile from now on.

The guy is unhinged. There's no telling what he'll do when he feels threatened.

But I did tell him the truth. I'm no cheater. I'm only doing this for the money and not to fuck his fiancé.

The money is all I care about.

# 16

*ANNA*

ANOTHER DAY OF WORK. Done.

I start to collect my things from my desk, dumping them in my bag. And that's when I spot the wrapped present next to my chair.

*Oh. That.*

I've completely forgotten about Chase's present.

I've tried to blank out that whole incident this morning from my mind. It was so awkward seeing both him and my fiancé together like that. Talking. Staring each other down. And then Angus *actually* went into the elevator with Chase, and at that moment, it felt like my whole body was shaking. Anxiety rocked my entire core. I didn't know what they talked about, but Angus emerged from the elevator a few minutes later looking shellshocked.

They must've really come to verbal blows.

Angus didn't even talk to me. He just stormed off back to his office.

Shit must've really hit the fan.

*Ugh. Great.*

The whole dance lesson thing was a big mistake. I should never have gone to it. I should never have agreed to it. I should've walked straight out of that first lesson properly when I saw who my teacher was going to be. I should've known it'll end badly.

*Well, today's the last day you're ever going to see Chase, Anna.*

And I'm glad about it.

Now to get rid of his present somehow.

Like hell I'm going to open it.

"Anna!"

I spin around. It's Erin. She's snuck up behind me.

I hope she hasn't spotted the present.

"Oh, hey."

"I haven't seen you all day," she says.

"Yeah. I've been busy with a lot of crazy stuff, you know?"

"How are the dance lessons going? You had one last night, yeah?"

*I might as well tell her the truth now. Get it over with.*

"Yeah, I've been thinking about them," I reply softly. "And I've been thinking of giving them up."

The smile on Erin's face falls away. "Give up?" she asks.

"I think so. I don't think Chase and I are a... natural fit."

"A natural fit? He's just your teacher, not a new puppy."

"I can't do this. I can pay you for it all."

"You can't just give up, Anna."

"I'm sorry, Erin. It's just not meant to be. I don't think I suit that kind of dancing."

"Sure you do," my best friend replies. "Just give it another shot."

I think about Chase. About him going through my stuff. About him turning up to work today and surprising me.

*I don't want to see his arrogant ass again.*

"Thank you for organizing it all, Erin. But it's just not for me. I'll get you the money."

My friend looks crushed. I feel so bad. The look on her face seems like I'm rejecting her.

I mean, she did come up with the idea, but she's acting a bit too *upset* that I don't want to do it anymore. Like she's invested in it or something.

"If you want to," she says weakly.

*Damn, I really feel bad. I gotta make this up for her somehow.*

"How about we go for a drink right now?" I suggest eagerly. "We can go to that new place around the corner, the one we haven't tried yet. Come on, the first round is on me."

Erin shakes her head. "I'm busy tonight," she replies. "See you."

She quickly turns and ducks into the elevator. She's gone before I have a chance to apologize again.

*She really took that to heart. It's so unlike her.*

But I'm not doing another lesson with Chase. No way. Not after the way I caught him snooping around my stuff. It was rude of him to appear at my work like he did today. He's been too much of a cocky dick for my liking.

*It is tempting to open the present he gave me, though.*

I glance back at it under my desk.

Maybe.

No.

I won't.

I spot Angus approaching the elevator from down the hallway.

*Maybe he might be a bit more talkative than Erin.*

I skip up to him.

"Hey, Angus."

"Hi."

He barely looks at me.

"So, I was thinking we could go out for dinner tonight," I say. "It's a little spontaneous, I know. But we can go home and get ready, then head out. How does that sound? Go to one of our favorite places. Have a good night."

He doesn't even pause to consider it.

"Not tonight, babe. I've got clients to have dinner with."

"Oh, okay. No problem."

"I'll be home late."

Those are his last words to me before he disappears into the elevator. And then he's gone, just like Erin.

Leaving me all alone.

*Oh.*

I lean back against the reception desk. The office is empty now. Just me and my thoughts.

I really didn't want to be all by myself this evening, not after what happened last night. I just want some company to waste the night away and get out of my head.

*Screw it.*

I'll open Chase's goddamn present.

I bring the large square onto the desk and use my scissors to tear it open. I do it carefully as not to damage whatever he's got me.

And I gasp when I see it.

A blank white canvas.

*No way.*

Attached to the wrapping paper is a card. I rip it out.

*ANNA,*

*I can only apologize for what happened last night. It was wrong of me to look through your bag like that. I'm sorry.*

*But your painting was beautiful. And I'm not joking when I say that. I bet you're shaking your head right now at me, but I'm being serious. Have you ever considered going professional? Because you definitely should.*

*My mom was an artist. I haven't really told anyone else that. I grew up sitting in her bed watching her paint and draw all day. Seeing your painting yesterday reminded me of her. It's been a long time since I've thought of her in a positive way, so thank you. I guess.*

*If you really did make that painting I saw yesterday, then I think you have real talent. Please don't let it go to waste like my mom did.*

*Here's another canvas for you to play with.*

*Again, I'm sorry.*

*Captain Chase*

I LAUGH AT HIS SIGNATURE. Using his stripper name like that is so *him*.

Damn. He's good. He knows how to write a letter to make your soul soar.

I take another look at the blank canvas, then back at the card in my hands.

I'm going to have to do something about this.

## 17

*CHASE*

I wave at Stacy. She gives me a nod from across the bar, pulling out a beer from the fridge and breaking off the lid.

"Long day?" she asks, handing me the beer.

"Yep."

"I notice you haven't been back here to drink for a week."

She's right.

"Yep." I raise the cold bottle to my lips and take a long drink. "It's been a long week."

She gives me a weak smile and slides back down the bar to a customer. I slump on the stool, stuck in my head, ignoring the loud thudding music of the strip club around me.

It really has been a long week.

It's been a week since I appeared at Anna's office to hand her that apology-slash-present, and I haven't heard from her since. Her refusal to speak to me has been killing me up inside every single day. I didn't expect her silence to actually tie my stomach into knots like it has, but here we are.

Me. Captain Chase. I've never been affected by a girl like this before. Heck, I've never actually been affected by another *person* like this before. I've always thought of myself as a happy loner gliding through life without a care, a solitary shark happily swimming his own way through an ocean, but just a few days of silence from some chick has sent me crazy.

Anna's silence is *freaking* me out.

I take another sip of beer.

*What the hell's wrong with you, Chase?*

This isn't who I am.

I'm the guy who breaks hearts, not the guy who fawns over some girl who isn't even mine.

*I gotta get out of here. I gotta get out of my head. Ride my bike till dawn.*

I'm about to get up from the barstool when someone grabs my arm.

"You're Captain Chase, aren't you?"

I turn. It's a woman. I quickly scan her up and down. She's gorgeous, just my type. Big tits. Big ass. Just the girl to turn me on and keep me from getting lonely on a night like this.

"Yes, I am."

"You were so good tonight."

"Thank you."

"So *sexy*."

I smile.

"I try my best."

"Do you mind signing my ticket?" She asks, flicking up a ticket for the show tonight.

*Wow. I've never been asked that before. That's a first.*

"You want me to sign it?"

She flutters her eyelashes. "Yes please, I'm a big fan. I love watching you move."

"Alright. As long as you can get a pen."

*You're onto a winner here, Chase.*

She pulls out a sharpie. "Already prepared," she says. "I'm always prepared. For *anything*."

She bites her lip seductively and I smile. The woman is extremely flirty.

"Make it out to me," she says before I can put the pen to paper. "Make it out to Ruby."

"Nice name."

"Thanks."

I sign the ticket. I feel Ruby's eyes all over me as I do so, undressing me until I'm completely naked with her stare.

"Here."

She slowly takes the ticket from me, grazing my thumb with hers as she does so. We both lock eye contact. As we're looking at each other, she brings the ticket to her mouth, planting a long sloppy kiss on it.

I watch her in fascination.

She really is my type. I like women who know what they're doing. Women who know what they want.

But somehow my heart's not in it. For the first time in a long time, I'm simply not interested in a girl who's so obviously giving me *fuck me* eyes.

I'm only thinking about one thing. One person.

Anna Jensen.

*No. Get out of my head, Anna.*

Ruby takes the sharpie from me, placing the end of it between her lips and sucking on it.

"Now that I signed your ticket, will you do something for me?" I ask.

"Anything for the hottest man I've ever met."

*Oh, she's fun.*

"Write down your number," I say, sliding a napkin across the counter to her.

I don't feel invested in this, though. It's like I'm just going through the motions. I've gotten numbers from girls a billion times before, and this just feels like I'm on autopilot. I'm acting like a robot, executing pre-programmed moves from a time before I met Anna Jensen.

*Why can't I get her out of my mind? Why is her face the only thing I see?*

Ruby writes down her number on the napkin, shooting me a lustful look as she does so. That real *fuck me* look.

I know that, with one simple word from my lips, this girl will eagerly crawl into bed with me. I could have her right now. Usually, that would be enough for me.

Not tonight, though.

Finished with writing down her number, Ruby takes a step closer to me. Her big chest is practically brushing up against mine.

"Sometimes girls just want to have fun," she whispers. "I'm free right now to have some... *fun*."

*Damn, she's straight on it.*

I laugh. "Sorry, I've got plans now."

She pouts at me and wraps her hand around my neck. "You can't make time for a lady?"

I gently remove her hand. "Sorry, Ruby. Not tonight."

I take the napkin and hop off the stool.

I was lying. I have no plans tonight.

I don't know why I've refused her advances. Any other night I would've leaped at the chance to fuck her brains out. Rock her to her core.

But not tonight.

With a farewell nod at Stacy, I make my way out of Xstasy. Straight onto my motorcycle parked outside without a backward glance at Ruby.

I take a look down at the napkin, at the girl's number scrawled across it.

I rip it up. I throw the scraps into the gutter.

I know now why I refused Ruby's advances.

*Anna Jensen.*

My head's full of her.

* * *

SOMEBODY IS THERE outside my trailer when I pull up on my motorcycle. It's too dark to recognize them at first. I can only see a faint outline of them. It's only when I get off my bike, fists ready to attack if they're a threat, that I see who they are.

And my body stops still.

It's her.

*Anna Jensen.*

She stands, leaning against my trailer next to the front door. It's definitely her. She's not a ghost. She's not an apparition.

It's really her. Leaning outside my trailer.

"How do you know where I live?" I ask her as I collect my shit from my bike. I try to act nonchalant, like I'm not surprised to see her, but inside I'm boiling. I'm both excited and nervous at the same time.

And I never feel nervous.

She smiles at me. "I'm not stupid. I went to your club and spoke to Toby, your boss."

I snort. "Toby isn't my boss."

"Well, he gave me your address."

"He did that? The bastard. How did you manage that?"

"I can be very... persuasive when I want to be."

"I can imagine," I reply, heading to my trailer's front door. "What are you doing here?"

She pauses. She purses her lips together. She's careful of what she's about to say. "I wanted to see you. To talk to you about last week."

"Last week? I thought you never wanted to see me again."

"Things have changed."

I sigh. I unlock my trailer door. "Come inside."

She follows me into my home. I never let anyone else in here, especially a girl, but I guess Anna's an exemption to a lot of things in my life. I also thought I'll never teach dancing to someone. I also thought I would leap at the chance to screw any girl I met at a bar. I also thought I'd never think about a girl so much that my heart hurts. I guess Anna is the exemption to all of those things.

"Nice place," she says as she looks around, her eyes darting about.

"Don't lie," I reply.

"No, it's true. I like it. There's not much here. You don't own much material stuff, do you?"

"Don't say it's *minimalistic*. I hate that term."

She laughs. "You caught me."

"I just live how I want to live."

"Sounds nice. I wish I could have that."

"It's not much," I reply. "But it's home. For now."

"For now?"

"I like to keep myself always ready to be on the move. I like to move around, never spend too long in one place."

"How long's too long?"

Anna seems curious. Like, *seriously* curious and not just making small talk. I'll indulge her.

"Depends."

"Depends on what?"

"How I feel. Might be a year, might be two. I just see what I feel like. Then, if I want to, I just pack up all my stuff in an hour and be out of here on that motorcycle outside."

"That's kinda cool. I like that," she says.

"You like it?"

"Yeah. My life is the complete opposite of that. I've barely made it out of this city."

"You've never been traveling?" I ask her in disbelief.

"Only with my parents. And even then, it was staying at luxury hotels and going to expensive restaurants."

"Oh, boohoo. Such a *struggle*."

"Shut up," she giggles. "No, it just didn't feel like real traveling, you know? I want to feel like I've seen somewhere, *lived* somewhere, breathe the air. Not just the inside of a Hilton."

"Maybe you should get a motorcycle, Anna. Become a biker girl."

She chuckles again. "Maybe that's just what I need."

An awkward silence falls on us. I quickly try to break it by ducking down to the fridge. "Beer?" I ask. "Coffee?"

"I'm fine with water."

I pour her a glass.

"But what about connections?" she asks as she takes the water from me. "Friends? Do you not have anyone?"

I shrug. "I like to be on my own."

"You need someone in your life, though. You shouldn't be lonely. What about a girl?"

There's another awkward silence. We're getting good at these.

I crack open a beer for myself.

*Why am I being so weird around a girl? I'm not smooth, as usual. Your game's off today, Chase.*

"Thanks for the present," she eventually says.

"You like it?"

She blinks. "Yeah."

"Good. I didn't know if a canvas was right or not," I reply.

*Why are we so goddamn stilted?*

"No, it's perfect."

"Great."

"You never told me about your mother being a painter."

"I don't really tell anyone about her," I reply. "She wasn't the best mother to me."

"Really? That's sad."

"I can't blame her, though. I was a bit of a handful."

"A bit? I can imagine." She giggles. "What was she like?"

I feel uncomfortable talking about her, so I skip the topic. "I am sorry, though. For snooping through your bag. I didn't mean..."

Anna cuts me off with a wave of her hand. "I'm sorry too, for my crazy reaction. Of course, you saw the painting when my bag was open. I overreacted. I shouldn't have accused you of trying to steal money."

I smile. "So, does this mean you're back on for lessons?"

She smiles back. "Maybe."

"Next Tuesday then?"

"Yep, next Tuesday."

"This time I want you to come dressed as a cowgirl."

"A cowgirl?"

"Yep. A sexy cowgirl."

"Oh god. Why?"

I take a sip of beer. "You'll see."

## 18

*ANNA*

IT'S BEEN a few weeks since I've moved into Angus' place, but it still feels weird calling it home.

It doesn't feel like home.

I unlock the front door of his penthouse apartment and step inside.

It's very different from Chase's trailer.

Angus' place looks straight out of a generic catalog. Modern furnishings. Minimal furniture. No artwork. No sense of personality.

I walk into the vast open-plan living room. Angus is there, standing with his back to me, looking out over the view of the city. My family's skyscraper where we work looms up in the distant skyline. Intimidating.

"Hey Chase," I say as I hang my bag on the hook. "How was your dinner?"

He's been having a lot of dinners with clients the last week. He doesn't like talking work with me, so I can only guess that all these dinners must mean he's close to a big deal with these clients. I hope he isn't stressed.

My fiance turns around from the window.

His face is blank.

"Where have you been?" he asks.

"Oh, you know. Out doing things."

"I came home to you not here," he says.

"I was busy doing stuff."

"Where were you?"

I can hear the rising anger in his voice. I brace myself. He's in one of his moods. I know them too well.

There's no point in lying to him. Not when he's like this.

"I was with Chase. I thought you knew Tuesdays are my dance lesson night."

Angus shakes his head. "Fucking Chase," he mutters under his breath. "You were out with him?"

"Yeah, for my regular dance lesson."

"You were out without telling me, with him?"

"Yeah, well, he *is* my teacher."

"With *him?*"

I raise my hands. "What are you insinuating here, Angus?"

"I'm not insinuating anything," he replies. "Why are you so defensive about you and this Chase guy?"

"I'm not being defensive. I'm just confused by what you think of me."

He sighs.

"I'm confused as to why you weren't home tonight."

"Am I not allowed to do my own thing?" I ask.

"If you're playing around my back, then no."

"Do you think Chase and I have something going on?"

There's a long pause.

"Do you?" he asks.

"Of course not. I'm not a cheater. I will never cheat on you, Angus."

"I don't believe you."

"Well, you have to believe me," I reply. "He's just my dance teacher."

"How dare you go somewhere without telling me."

"What do you want me to do? Let you track me on GPS every hour of every day?" I ask.

"That might be a good idea. I might be able to trust you a bit then."

He's actually being serious.

"How many times do I have to tell you that you can trust me? How many times do I have to say that I will never, ever cheat on you?"

Angus doesn't reply. He storms away towards the bedroom. I follow him inside. He sits down on the bed.

And I sit down next to him.

"I don't want us to go to sleep angry with each other. I want you to know that I will never be unfaithful to you, Angus," I say softly. And I mean it.

He doesn't even look at me.

I lean towards him. My lips graze his neck. I start to kiss him, seductively bringing my hands around him. My fingers brush over his skin. I feel on fire. I'm on a roll here. This is great. This is all coming effortlessly to me.

*Wow, Chase's lessons really are working.*

I feel sexy. I feel confident in how I use my body. I'm in the groove. I feel like I can do anything, that I'm no longer ashamed of my body.

Those dance lessons have really changed me for the better.

And now I just want Angus. I want my fiancé. I feel a passion inside me needing to burst out.

I want to fuck my fiancé so much.

"I love you," I whisper into his ear. I begin to nibble at it.

He still doesn't look at me.

Time to bring out the big guns. I flip over onto him, sitting on his lap flirtatiously, wrapping my legs around his waist. I bring my head in close to his, kissing his jawline.

I'm turned on. I want to be satisfied. I want to satisfy my soon-to-be husband.

But then he's pushing me away. His hands are cold. He unwraps my legs from around him, leaning me back away from his face.

"I don't want you touching me when you've touched another man," he says coldly.

My mouth practically hits the floor.

"What are you saying? I love you, Angus. No man has touched me since we've been together."

"How do I know you love me?"

I start to choke up.

*Why is he saying these things? Can't he see that I'm right here, in front of him, giving him my all?*

"I do love you, Angus. I really do. I want to make us work."

"How can I trust you?"

"You can. We're engaged. I love you." I repeat it again. Desperately. "I love you."

"They're just words."

He pulls himself up from the bed and walks directly into the en-suite. He shuts the door. A minute later, I hear the shower running.

I fall back on the bed, tears welling in my eyes.

*How can he believe I'm cheating on him?*

Is this what our marriage is going to be? Silences and unfounded accusations?

I don't know what to think.

I just lie on the bed in the rich empty penthouse as the shower runs in the other room and I begin to cry.

# 19

*ANNA*

I OPEN the door to the dance studio.

Chase is already there. He's standing in full cowboy garb. The hat. The boots. He's just missing a shirt.

I realize it's been the first time I've seen him topless since the night we met.

And he looks amazing.

I bite my lip.

"You're early. For once," I say as I enter.

He spins around to face me, a wide smile on his face.

"And you've actually turned up," he replies. "I guess each of us is full of surprises."

I dump my bag next to his.

"We'll see for how long."

"I promise this is going to be good," he replies.

"Okay. So... cowgirl outfit."

Chase raises his eyebrows.

"You did bring it, did you?" he asks.

I take in a deep breath. "Yep. It's just..."

"Come on, spit it out."

"I don't know if it's my thing..."

Chase's face lights up.

"Exactly," he says. "That's what makes it perfect for you. Putting it on will push you out of your comfort zone."

"Really?" I'm so unsure.

Especially when I see him like this, all dressed up. He looks great, whilst I'm afraid I'm going to look like a kid dressing up at a birthday party.

"Of course." Chase nods towards the bathroom door. "Go and put it on."

"I don't know."

"It's only me in here."

"And the mirrors," I point out.

"Yep, those too," Chase laughs. "They can't hurt you. Now, shut up and go put it on."

I sigh reluctantly. "Alright."

I carry my stuff into the bathroom and get changed into the cowgirl outfit. I look at myself in the mirror once dressed and laugh at the state I'm in. I did try to go for sexy cowgirl, but I think I've accidentally veered into looking like Jessie from the *Toy Story* movies.

"You look ridiculous, Anna," I say softly at my reflection.

I gulp.

Time to face Chase's laugh.

And I won't blame him. I look stupid.

*Why did you think you could pull this off?*

"Yep, this is definitely out of my comfort zone," I say as I step out back into the dance studio. I throw up my arms and look down at the outfit, displaying it for him to see.

I brace myself for Chase's laugh, but it doesn't come. Instead, his eyes travel up and down me as if he's carefully inspecting. Serious.

It's like he's checking out a new car.

"You look good," he eventually says. "Well done."

I let out my breath.

*That was not the reaction I was expecting.*

"You don't think it's too much?" I ask.

"You might be uncomfortable in it, but I reckon you look great," Chase replies. "It's just what you need."

"Yeah?"

"Yep."

"Alright, if you say so."

I'm still so hesitant.

"Take a seat. Watch what I do," Chase tells me before he turns on the music. A remixed country song blares through the speaker system as I sit down.

Chase starts to strip. His body moves in time to the music. He tilts his cowboy hat at me before thrusting with his crotch. The man really can move. I'm taken back to that night six months ago as he starts to remove his clothes in front of me again.

Then he pulls out a rope tied into a lasso.

I swallow.

*Oh, God. Not this.*

He's doing the full cowboy routine, I see.

And it's kinda hot.

He smirks before he throws the lasso over me, trapping me in the chair, my arms pinned to my sides. He slides towards me slowly, tugging at the rope seductively.

*God, this is very hot.*

I'm tied up by the rope as Chase approaches me, his muscles bulging under the light.

He spins around, flashing me his ass in his tight denim jeans.

I whoop, encouraging him even further.

He continues his routine.

"Don't milk this," I say to him as he throws his hat towards me.

Chase laughs. "I see what you did there. *Milk*. Cowboy."

"Oh, I can be cheesy too, you know," I reply, grinning.

This whole situation is hilarious; I just have to laugh.

"See?" He asks, turning off the music. "That's what you need to do. Get the blood boiling."

\* \* \*

WE DANCE for the next hour, Chase showing me all the moves. He teaches me how to use the lasso. I squeal as the rope flies across the room when I attempt to throw it over the stripper. Tie him up like he did to me.

It's so much fun.

And really, really hot.

And soon the lesson is over.

"That was actually really good today," I say to Chase as we pass the studio reception out the front doors. "I might even use some of those moves in the bedroom with Angus."

"So, you don't regret coming back?" he asks.

"Nope. Do you?"

He turns to me. "Nope."

"Even when I can be such a bitch?"

"You're not too bad."

"So, you've actually dealt with worse?"

He chuckles. "You should meet my trailer park manager. She'll give you a run for your money."

He opens the front door for me.

"Thanks for the canvas again," I say, emerging into the evening air.

"No problem."

I might as well ask the question that's been annoying me all week.

"So, your mother's an artist?"

"She was."

*Was?*

"Oh, did she stop?"

"She passed away," Chase says softly.

"I'm sorry. I didn't know."

*Damn, Anna. Wrong move.*

"Don't be. It happened a long time ago when I was sixteen. I ran away soon after. No way was I going to get caught up in the whole adoption and foster home system. And I've been running ever since, I suppose. I was pretty torn up about her for a very long time. It took me ages to finally get over it. I spent years running, searching for a purpose, but I couldn't find one. I worked odd jobs all over the country until I did stripping, and since then I've never looked back."

He speaks in one long go. It's like he's never said these things out loud. It's like I'm the first person he's talked to about his life. Maybe I am. I wonder how many people he's told his story to.

I reach out for his arm. "I am sorry about your mother."

"It's nothing."

He looks at me so intensely that I have to spin away.

"So, that's your bike?" I ask, pointing at the parked motorcycle.

Chase leaps over the back of it. "Yeah, she's my baby."

"You call it your baby?"

"Don't snigger. She treats me well."

"What do you think you're in?" I ask, laughing. "A music video for Bruce Springsteen's *Thunder Road*?"

"You laugh, but chicks dig this."

"I bet they do."

"Oh, they love a bad boy on a bike."

"And is that what you are?"

He winks. "You know me."

I don't want to admit it, but his motorcycle *is* hot.

"Well, see you next week, biker boy."

Chase smiles and revs up the motorcycle. "See you, cowgirl."

## 20

*CHASE*

"THIS IS MY SIGNATURE LOOK," I say to Anna as I show off my body.

She looks at me up and down with her face scrunched up. She's clearly mocking me.

"Oh, I know, *Captain* Chase," she replies. "Yep. Your *signature* look."

*I'm glad she gets it.*

"Exactly," I reply. "Call me Captain."

Anna rolls her eyes.

But she doesn't have me fooled; I know she's actually secretly loving this.

Girls always like to pretend that they're exasperated with my witty humor, but they all secretly love it. And Anna is no exception.

It's another week of dance lessons, and this time we're standing in the middle of the studio wearing army costumes.

Hence the Captain in my name.

Like I said to Anna, it's my signature look.

I've got the full gear on. A tight pale green vest. Short khaki shorts. An army beret fitted on my head.

The full military look that drives women mad.

"Girls like a man in uniform," I say proudly with my hands on my hips, showing off my large biceps bulging out of my army vest. "I think I look good."

For the second time today, Anna rolls her eyes at me.

She stands in front of me, also dressed for the Army. The sexy Army.

"You think a lot of things, Chase. Not all of them are true."

"How about you say that to all the women I've happily satisfied? I bet they all think I look good."

She raises an eyebrow at me. "And how do you know they're satisfied?"

"Oh, it's obvious. I've done it plenty of times."

"Women can fake it."

"Not with me," I reply.

She laughs. "I bet at least half the women you've been with have faked it."

"Bullshit."

"It isn't."

"I think I'm different from a lot of men," I reply. She's really starting to bruise my ego now. "I know how to do things to women."

"Chase, just because you can move your body and you've worked out a lot doesn't mean you're any different from any other man."

"So, you do admit I look pretty good?"

Again, she rolls her eyes, but she can't stop laughing.

I like it when she laughs.

"This one somehow feels even more uncomfortable than the one last week," she says, trying to adjust her pants around her ass area. "I can't believe you've made me dress up like this. I feel like I'm disrespecting the military somehow."

"Oh, trust me, Anna, Army women love this. If not more than civilians."

She stares at me. "I'll just have to take your word for it."

"Why else do you think my name is Captain Chase? This is my best routine."

"I think your name is Captain Chase because you're an unfunny dullard who's crap at puns."

I mime getting shot. "That's the worst thing you've ever said to me, Anna. My puns are my proudest achievements," I reply.

She laughs. "You really have to work on them."

"I'm actually surprised by your commitment here," I say.

"Commitment?"

I wave at her uniform.

"Being able to pick out some good stripper gear. It's impressive."

She winks. "I've got plenty of talents."

"And soon you'll be able to add dancing to your list."

"I dunno," she replies. "I just don't think my fiancé would be super into my stripping for him, especially not in your cheesy way."

"I'll ignore you calling it *cheesy*. But sure, maybe he won't like it, maybe he will. You've just got to try it. And besides, this is not all about just taking your clothes off. I'm actually teaching you how to *move*."

She thinks about it for a second. "You're right," she replies. "I don't know why I ever doubted the abilities of the great Captain Chase."

"Now stand to attention," I bark. Giggling, Anna does so. I stare at her, stony-faced, before marching around her to inspect her posture.

Anna stands completely still, but I can see the laughter behind her eyes threatening to burst out.

I, on the other hand, am taking this role-play very seriously.

"Very good, soldier."

"Thanks, Chase."

*She's being cheeky.*

"Did I tell you to speak, private?" I shout, getting my face right up into Anna's. "You'll speak only when commanded to. You got that?"

"Yes, sir."

Oh, by the look on her face, Anna is enjoying playing along as well.

"And you shall only refer to me as Captain or sir, you understand?"

"Yes, captain."

"Good. Now I want you to jog on the spot. Build up some sweat for me."

Anna eagerly launches into it, her legs jumping up and down as she runs on the spot. She immediately starts building up a sweat. Her forehead glistens.

"I like to see this, soldier," I say. "Very good."

"Thank you, sir."

"Now that you're all sweaty, strip for me."

"With what routine?" she asks.

"Make one up, private. Adapt to the situation and improvise like a real soldier."

"Yes, sir."

I switch the music to a military drill. I sit back and watch as Anna starts to dance. She tears out of her Army outfit. Slowly she thrusts her crotch, just like I've shown her how. She runs her fingers to her mouth, sucking on them greedily.

She's getting real good at this.

It's amazing to see how in a few weeks she's gone from a shy timid snob to this energetic, confident goddess.

*She sure has one hell of a lucky fiancé, especially when I'm all done with her.*

"Very good, soldier. Lesson over."

\* \* \*

"So, THAT PAINTING WAS YOURS?" I ask, standing outside the bathroom as Anna gets changed back into her regular clothes.

"What painting?"

I can't see her past the door. She has to raise her voice.

"The one in your bag," I reply.

"Oh, yeah. I painted that one."

"You really did?"

"Yeah."

"You should go pro."

Anna laughs like I'm joking. Like it's the stupidest idea she's ever heard.

"I'm being serious," I rebuke. "You totally should try to become a professional at this. That painting is great."

"Maybe in another life," she replies.

"What does that mean?"

There's a long pause. The door opens, and she steps out.

Anna Jensen is a very pretty woman. Every time I see her, my heart stops. I can't help it.

She's beautiful.

*But she's also getting married, Chase. You don't like cheaters. You don't want to get used by a married woman again.*

But she isn't just another spoiled rich girl, not from what I've seen in the last few weeks. I had her pegged completely wrong that time I met her again in the dance studio. She's more than just another one like Alice. Her passion for painting proves it.

"I've never really told anyone," she says as she emerges from the bathroom, locking eyes with me and smiling in her sweet way that makes my heart stop again. "But painting professionally is my dream. It's just a shame that the... life I lead doesn't lend itself well to artistic pursuits."

I shrug. "If it's what you love doing, then screw everything else. Do what you want to do."

"That might be easy for you to say," Anna replies, looking me up and down. "With your leather jackets and your motorcycle and your carefree life. Not all of us can be free."

"Yes, you can."

"Trust me, when you come from my family, nothing is ever your choice."

"Boohoo, you're rich. Big deal."

"Everything in life comes with a price," Anna replies sternly. "I've got responsibilities. *Expectations*. Not all of us can just ride into the sunset like you."

"But you do have a choice," I say. "We all have a choice. Stick with the plan others have designed for us or choose our own path in life."

She shakes her head. "You say it so simply, but it's harder than that."

"It isn't hard."

She glares at me. "You wouldn't know."

I raise my hands. "I've built up my own life. I'm happy. I get to do what I love. Why can't you?"

"You don't know the people I know. You don't have my family."

"So? You can't let others control you."

"It really is not as simple as that, Chase."

"I believe in you," I say. "I believe in your ability. Forget what other people say. You have the talent to go professional. If only you put time and effort into it."

Anna's cheeks blush. Her head darts away from me as I tell her she's talented.

*I bet no one in her life had ever had faith in her before.*

"I best be getting home," she says. "My fiance will be waiting."

And then we walk to the building's exit, not speaking another word. She leaves, and I stand there on the steps of the dance studio, watching her go.

## 21

*ANNA*

DAD'S ACTUALLY, surprisingly, on time at the restaurant. I don't have to wait long sitting at the table when I see him stroll through the front doors with the confident swagger only reserved for a billionaire.

"Hello, sweetheart," he says as he pecks me on the cheek. I beam at him. All day I had been nervous about him coming tonight, thinking that I was forcing him to do this. But Dad, being on time, means that he does actually want to be here.

*It's a first.*

"Thank you for taking the time to have dinner with me," I say as I take the seat opposite him at the table.

Dad waves away my concerns with a casual flick of his wrist. His luxury Rolex flashes under the restaurant lights. "I am happy you booked us in here. It's always good to have some precious father-daughter time."

"Exactly," I reply. "It is good for us to just talk privately."

I exhale in relief. It seems like I've caught him at a perfect moment. He's not in one of his infamous bad moods.

The truth is that I've invited him out for dinner because I want to ask him something. Dad and I barely have private dinners or even private conversations anymore, not since I was a little girl, but something's been eating away at me for the last few days and I want to let it out.

And it's all to do with what Chase said to me in our last dance lesson. All about how I should try to go professional with my painting. About how I should pursue my passion in life.

*I hope he takes this well.*

Although there's a voice in the back of my head saying it's obvious he won't.

The waiter appears by our side. Dad orders the restaurant's most expensive bottle of wine.

*Typical Dad.*

"How's Angus?" my father asks me once the waiter disappears to get our drink.

I nod. "He's fine."

"Fine?"

"We're in love," I hasten to reassure him.

"You're marrying a good boy there, Anna. Trust me. You have a good future ahead with him."

"Well, you're the one who recommended him."

He leans back. "I did. I do have great taste."

"He's been very busy with work recently," I say. "He seems to be inundated with a lot of clients in the last few weeks."

Dad frowns. "I've actually lessened his workload to give you two more time together after your engagement," he says. "He shouldn't be busy at all."

"Really?"

"But maybe he's ignoring me and finding more work for

our company on the side. Good man. He shows initiative. I like that. He'll definitely make a fine husband for you, Anna."

I'm about to say something in return, something along the lines of how Angus had told me specifically that Dad had given him these clients to deal with, but already our waiter has reappeared with the bottle of red wine Dad had requested. He pours two drinks, and by the time Dad and I chink our glasses, I've already forgotten what my father has said about Angus.

"I must admit," Dad says as he places his wine back down. "When I saw my secretary had put this dinner into the diary, I thought there'd been a mistake."

"No mistake."

"Is there any particular reason you want to see me tonight?" he asks quietly.

He knows something's up. My dad's a smart man.

*I might as well say it now.*

I shift nervously in my seat. "I did want to talk about something."

His eyebrow lifts.

"Oh? Do tell."

"Well, actually, I wanted to talk about painting."

"Painting? You want to get into the art dealer business?" Dad chuckles.

I'm doing this because I want his approval. Maybe he could see a few paintings I've done and change his mind. I just want my dad to reaffirm my talent, that's all I want.

That's all I've ever wanted from him.

"Actually, I'm more talking about how I used to love painting as a teenager."

Dad grunts and scratches his chin. "Not this again."

"I was thinking about picking it up again. Trying my hand at it. You see, I have a friend review an old painting of mine the other day and he thinks it might be good enough..."

Dad raises his hand, and I already know I've spoken too far.

I sit back in my seat and bite my lip, waiting for what's coming.

"Let me tell you something here, Anna," Dad says, leaning across the table towards me. "Let me give you some kind father-daughter advice before you start blabbering on."

*I shouldn't have done this. I shouldn't have asked for this dinner.*

I was just looking for Dad's love.

But now he's going to berate me.

"You're about to be married to Angus," Dad continues. You need to be a good wife for him and ignore any bizarre passions you have."

"But painting makes me happy."

*Why am I still trying to get through to him?*

"What even is happiness?" Dad asks rhetorically. "It's an obscure concept. But *marriage*? Marriage is stable. A good, sensible marriage brings order. That's happiness. Happiness is not throwing away the potential of your life in strange artistic pursuits."

"I can always do it part time," I suggest hopelessly.

"Do you think Angus will stay with you if you spend all your time painting and not attending to his needs? No."

"But..."

"Forget about it," Dad interrupts me again. I see his face turning pink. He's losing his cool. "Follow the example of your mother, Anna. When I met her, she was into cooking."

"Cooking?"

"She had some wild thoughts of being a chef."

I blink. "I didn't know that."

"Exactly," Dad replies. "When she married me, I told her to stop all that. I told her to get out of the restaurant."

"I never knew she wanted to be a chef," I say softly.

"Believe me, Angus won't stick around if he isn't your number one priority. Be like your mother."

"She really wanted to work in a kitchen?"

It's so strange, I've never seen her care for anything in life. She's never had anything she was crazy for. Dad must've really forced that out of her.

"It was too messy. I couldn't have her running around town doing dirty work like that with men I didn't know."

"But what if she was happy doing it?" I ask quietly.

"She's happier now, trust me," Dad replies, his face cold. "Marriage made her happy. She has a roof over her head and three meals a day. She'll never have to worry about money for the rest of her life. You should look at what she did. Be like her, for Angus."

"Be like Mom and give up my one passion?"

"Trust me, you don't want your fiancé to leave you. You don't want to end up unmarried in your thirties."

I bow my head and drink my wine. I don't raise the topic anymore for the rest of tonight. I just sit back, eat my food, and listen to Dad talk about his work.

I feel numb. Empty.

What can you do when even your own parents don't support you? Combined with Angus's coldness, I just feel so alone.

It's only when I'm in the taxi home after saying good-night to Dad that I let myself cry. And I don't stop until I reach home.

# 22

*ANNA*

I PULL the glasses off my nose and seductively bite on the end of it. I wrap my lips around the plastic and begin to suck.

I run my hands through my hair, leaning my head back and emitting a soft moan.

My hands travel down my neck, unbuttoning my blouse. My tits spill out, but still constrained by my bra though.

"Very good," Chase remarks, nodding his head in approval. "You're great at playing a saucy secretary."

He has to talk loud to be heard over the thudding music that's playing. I feel like I'm in a film. Some film that's very raunchy and only found on the internet.

And it's making me *pretty* horny.

I stand up, straightening my tight pencil skirt. "Well, I practically have to be a saucy secretary at work every day," I reply. "You could say I've had plenty of practice."

Chase turns around and turns off the music. "Exactly,"

he says. "This scenario is close to home for you. You know the world of a secretary inside and out. It could be your best asset in the bedroom with your fiance. Do you both play dress up?"

I blink, taken aback by his direct question. I blush. "No... not really."

*We don't even have sex often. Angus hasn't touched me in weeks.*

"Well, this might help spice things up. Play the saucy secretary. We sometimes feel our most sexy when we turn the things most familiar to us on their head."

"Okay."

Maybe Chase is right, maybe dressing up in this fun and sexy way will make Angus interested in me.

I hope so because I'm really feeling lost now.

My fiancé doesn't respond to me at all. Every night he's asleep or uninterested. No amount of persuasion from me even budges him.

I've just been proposed to, but I feel all alone at the one point in my life when I should feel the most love.

At least I have Chase's dance lessons to look forward to each week. They're the one thing that keeps me going.

"I mean, look at me," Chase says, glancing down at the businessman suit he's wearing. "The only time I ever dress like this is when I'm stripping."

I giggle. He does look so strange all done up in a jacket and tie. Tucked in shirt and everything.

"You're like a little businessman," I remark. "A little boy off to school."

He narrows his eyes at me. "*Little?*"

"You heard me."

He switches on the music and starts to dance, loosening his tie and ripping off the suit buttons to reveal his muscular chest. All as if to prove how *not* little he is.

I laugh and follow him, getting to my feet and dancing wildly. I'm not even bothered about stripping. I'm just free with the music. I'm shaking out all the stresses in my life. For one glorious moment, I'm experiencing pure joy, unrestrained by all the doubts and fears plaguing my head. The music moves through me. I'm just simply *dancing*.

I'm free.

I don't realize that my teacher has stopped moving and has been watching me the whole time. If I did, I would see the smile beaming across his face.

Chase winds down the music and turns to me.

I stop, panting. Surprised by even my own energy.

I brush my wild hair back. "I lost myself there for a moment," I say, exhausted.

*That was pretty liberating.*

"I think you're ready," Chase says.

I narrow my eyes. "What do you mean? Ready for what?"

"I think you're ready for the big leagues."

"The big leagues? What's that?"

Chase winks at me. "Club Xstasy."

"What?"

"I think you're ready to get on stage there."

I gasp. Not the club. "No, no, no, no."

I'm pretty empathetic, but Chase ignores my protestation.

"I think it'll be good for you. I'll book you in for next week."

"Next week?" I can't hide the horror in my voice.

"Don't worry, we're going to go over it a billion times. We're going to rehearse all week."

"No, Chase."

"Every night."

"No."

"Right here. We'll practice together. It'll be great."

"No."

"Bring your fiancé along. Let him see the work you've done."

"No."

"It might add some spice to your love life."

I'm adamant. "No, Chase."

He smiles. He's completely unfazed by my rejection.

"Oh, you're doing it, Anna. You can't get out of this one."

"No. Way."

He strolls across the dance studio and stands, cross-armed, at the door.

"I'm not letting you leave until you confirm you'll do it," he says, smirking.

"This is technically kidnapping," I reply.

"I don't care. You're staying here until you decide to do a routine with me at Xstasy next week."

"No."

"Yes."

"*No.*"

"Yes."

He's so goddamn confident I'll do it.

*And I know he's right.*

Against my better judgment, I know I'm going to do it.

"Fine," I say, exasperated.

"Fine?"

"I'll do your stupid routine."

He bares his white teeth in a perfect smile. "Lovely."

I sigh.

Oh, God. I'm going to *strip* on a stage. In front of an audience.

# 23

*ANNA*

I TAKE in a deep breath before I enter Angus's - *my* - apartment.

My fiancé is standing in the kitchen, drinking a bottle of beer, when I walk in. He sneers at the sight of me.

*What have I done to piss him off like this?*

Every day since the proposal, it's like he's getting worse. Like there's a widening gulf between us.

"How was your lesson?" he asks.

I shrug. "It was good."

He stays silent for a long time, just staring at me. He clearly isn't happy.

"How many more lessons do you have with this guy?" he eventually asks.

I lean against the kitchen counter opposite him. "Well, that's the thing I was meaning to tell you tonight, Angus. I'm going to be in a show."

He sips his beer, eyeing me suspiciously. "A show?"

I take in another deep breath, tensing for what's about to come.

"I'm going to be performing at a club next week, so I'll be rehearsing every night until then, if you don't mind."

"I do mind."

I ignore his comment and continue.

"I would love it if you came and see me dance. I really feel like I've improved so much in the last few weeks. I think you'll really like it."

"*You think I'll like it?* You think I'll like to see you strip naked on a stage in front of other people?"

"It's not like that at all. It's for women. I bet you'll be the only guy there. And I don't even get naked. It's more like a dance," I reply, my voice wavering.

"Pfft. A *dance*," he mutters under his breath.

"I've even booked you a table for you to come and watch me."

It's like I've told him I'm fucking his dad. "You've booked me a table?"

"I want you to be there for me," I say. "This means a lot."

"It means a lot to you, doesn't it? Well, what about me? Do you ever think about me? About what I want?"

"It's not like that."

"Then what is it, exactly?" Angus asks, slamming his bottle of beer down on the counter. The noise makes me jump. "You fucking other men, and now you want me to watch you do that?"

"I'm not fucking other men..."

"You think I'm some kind of *cuckold*? That I'll enjoy watching you whoring yourself out in a club?"

Tears are already forming in my eyes. "It's not like that at all, Angus. I would never cheat on you. It's a professionally choreographed routine."

"Choreographed my ass."

"Come and watch it. For me. Then you'll see what it's like. Give it a chance."

Angus shakes his head and turns away from me.

"You never do what I want you to do," he says under his breath.

And then Dad's words come to me.

*Do you think Angus will stay with you if you spend all your time painting and not attending to his needs?*

Is this what's happening now?

I'm terrified. I'm losing my fiancé right in front of my eyes. He doesn't even trust me to make my own decisions. He doesn't even trust that I'm not cheating on him.

Are these the foundations of what our marriage is going to be based on?

"When you're out there, stripping yourself for cash like a slut," Angus says. "I will be here. Sitting in my apartment."

"Please come. You'll see it's not like that at all."

I'm practically begging him now. Tears are running down my cheeks.

"I think I'll be sleeping on the couch tonight," Angus mutters. He walks out of the kitchen and out of sight. I don't see him again for the rest of the night. I fall asleep alone.

*What has happened?*

Is my marriage crumbling apart before it's even begun?

# 24

*CHASE*

I CAN TELL Anna is nervous the minute she opens the door to my dressing room. I've just knocked to come in, double-checking it's safe for me to do so. She's been getting changed into her army outfit in there whilst I stand outside. And when she does open the door, fully dressed in her tight khaki uniform, that's when I realize how nervous she really is.

Her nose twitches when she hears the roaring of the audience echoing down the club's backstage hallways as she cracks open the door. She bites her lip in the familiar way I know she does when she gets anxious.

I know so much about Anna Jensen now. Who wouldn't know so much about another person when you've literally spent weeks teaching them to dance? Getting to know every part of their body as you teach them to move. Know them fully inside and out as you guide their limbs.

Dancing together is one of the best bonding exercises on

the planet, and Anna Jensen and I have done a lot of dancing in a few weeks. A *hell* of a lot of bonding.

"You nervous?" I ask her with a smile, leaning against the doorframe of my dressing room.

Anna stares up at me, defiant. But her eyes give her concealed fear away. "Nope."

"You sure? You have every right to be. There's a big crowd tonight."

Bless her heart, she's trying her best to appear strong.

She doesn't have to hide anything from me, though.

"There's a... big crowd?" she asks, hesitant.

"Oh, I thought you weren't nervous," I reply, mocking her.

"Shut up." She playfully punches me. Like her, I'm also wearing an army outfit. We decided to stick to my trademark look and do an army theme tonight. We've been rehearsing the same routine for the last week in preparation for this show.

And Anna's been great. She has absolutely no reason to be nervous.

She's just very, *very* cute when she's like this.

"Don't worry, I can hold your hand," I say mockingly.

Anna glares at me. "You are not holding my hand, Chase. I'm doing this by myself."

I laugh. "Can't take a joke, jeez."

"Are you nervous?" she asks.

She lets me into the dressing room. I glance around at the familiar mirrors.

It's not the first time Anna's been in here.

"I'm not nervous," I reply.

"How are you not?"

"Years of it."

Although tonight shouldn't be any different from the

hundreds of shows I've done in the past, it somehow *feels* like it.

And I know why.

*Because Anna's with me.*

"You're warmed up?" she asks.

"Are you?"

"Yep."

I nod towards the door, where the music is blaring and the crowd's screams are overbearing.

"We're on next. We better get to the stage."

Anna pants.

"Oh, Jesus."

"I thought you said you weren't nervous?" I ask.

"I'm not."

"Right," I say suspiciously. I nod towards the dressing room bathroom. "Remember what we got up to in that room there?"

Anna is definitely in no mood for my jokes.

"Don't even mention that night again," she warns, pointing a wagging finger at me. "Don't you dare."

I laugh again and follow her out of the dressing room. Towards our fate.

\* \* \*

THE LAST ACT before us comes off stage.

How am I not surprised that it's Ryan doing his goddamn Tarzan routine? Yet again. He passes us in the hallway behind the stage. I roll my eyes at the sight of him in his ridiculous jungle outfit.

The announcer brushes past us to introduce our act to the crowd.

*Anna and Chase.*

"My fiancé doesn't approve of this," Anna whispers to me as I'm stretching against the wall.

"What do you mean?"

"He doesn't like what I'm doing," she says.

"Do *you* like what you're doing?" I ask.

She looks at me with a serious face. "I do."

"Then that's all that matters."

Anna nods slowly. "Thank you."

"Did you offer him tickets?"

She sighs, exasperated. "I booked him a whole table," she says.

"Oh, I'm sorry."

Anna shakes her head.

"Don't worry. I think he would've hated all this, anyway."

"You're not doing this for him," I reply. "You're doing this for you, and you alone. It's time to let your inner sex goddess out."

"Yeah."

"Enjoy yourself. This is going to be a once-in-a-lifetime experience."

"Sure."

"Listen to me," I say, reaching over to cup Anna's chin in my hand. I look her square in the eyes. "You're amazing. You've been amazing these last few weeks, and you'll be amazing up there on stage. I thought this whole little experiment of ours was going to be a total disaster at the beginning, but it's turned out to be the opposite. Anna, I am proud of you. I am so happy you've come back into my life."

A single tear rolls down her cheeks. "I'm happy too," she says quietly.

We can hear the announcer on stage yelling our names and we quickly straighten up, ready. It's like his voice reverberates around us through the microphone, rattling our very bones as he talks us up to the screaming crowd.

*We have a little something special for you all tonight. A debut performance. Our very own Captain Chase has been teaching her for this. It's an exclusive event, just for you lucky people tonight.*

Our music starts.

*Performing with our crowd favorite, it's the debut of Army Anna!*

The audience cheers.

And even I'm feeling the nerves now.

I wink at Anna. She smiles back at me.

She chose her stripper name. I'm glad she also went for alliteration, like mine. She might profess to hating my puns and silly names, but she chose this one for herself. My personality must be rubbing off on her.

"Let's give them one hell of a performance," I say. "Let's dance rough and dirty."

This time she isn't repulsed by the term, but is instead grinning with glee.

And then she nods. She's ready.

And we rush onto the stage.

# 25

*ANNA*

CHASE and I run off the stage, laughing uncontrollably. Laughing in joy.

"We actually did it," I excitedly yell to him as we stumble into the backstage darkness. "We actually frigging did it!"

We really had actually done it.

The army routine we'd so stressfully prepared over the last week was pulled off without a hitch up there on stage. Everything had gone according to plan.

*And it was glorious.*

I was so incredibly nervous backstage before we started. The roar of the crowd, the harsh lights, and the blaring music had nearly frozen me in place. I thought I wasn't even going to move, let alone dance.

But then we were forced on stage. Chase started the routine, and everything just fell into place.

I loved every minute of it. I didn't expect I would, but the whole experience was just damn fun.

The crowd of drunk women cheered and clapped along as I danced and ripped off my clothes. Chase and I moved together just as we had practiced. We were a team.

"You were fantastic," Chase tells me as we rush back into his dressing room. We're completely out of breath. I feel the adrenaline surge through me. I can't stop smiling.

"*You* were fantastic," I reply. "That was amazing."

He's all smiles too.

"I can't believe we pulled it off."

"You can't believe it? What about me?" I ask. "I didn't even think I could dance a few weeks ago."

Chase grabs my shoulders. Sweat pours off his face. He's breathing rapidly, his chest heaving. "But you've done it," he says. "You're a real stripper now."

"All thanks to you," I reply, laughing. "I guess I am a real stripper now."

"And you make a pretty damn good one."

I poke him in his chest. "I had a pretty good teacher, I must say."

"And I had a pretty good student," he chortles back at me.

My eyes widen.

"Oh, which actually reminds me," I exclaim.

I turn from him and head to the corner of the dressing room, where I've kept something hidden for this very moment. Chase frowns. He doesn't know what I've done.

*I've got him a present.*

I snuck it in backstage before the show and secretly placed it here.

I pick it up and pull it up so that it's in front of my chest. It's pretty unwieldy.

It is a large square. All wrapped up.

"What's this?" he asks.

"What do you think it is, stupid? It's a present," I reply.

"For me?"

"Who else for? It's to say thank you for the past seven weeks."

Chase shakes his head and collects the present from me. "You really don't have to do this," he replies softly.

*He's actually touched.*

"I just wanted to say thank you," I reply. "For everything."

He tears open the wrapping paper. I wait eagerly for the reaction on his face. It doesn't disappoint.

Chase practically gasps when he sees the present.

What I've done is taken the canvas he gifted me and painted it. I've painted an image of him riding his motorcycle in the desert. Wind lapping at his hair. He's looking like a true bad boy on a bike, just as I know he imagines himself to be.

I think it's the best painting I've ever done.

"What is this?" he asks, shocked, as he stares at the artwork.

"It's you."

"I can see that."

I smile.

*He really is taken aback by this.*

"You like it?" I ask, stepping beside him. He turns to me.

I think I can see tears in his eyes, or is that a trick of the light?

"Anna," he replies. "I *love* it."

And then he's kissing me.

It's completely spontaneous.

I'm completely floored by it.

*And I don't want it.*

It takes me a second to realize what's happening, a second of feeling my lips against his, and then I'm pushing back from him. My hands press on his chest, bringing my face away from his.

"What are you doing, Chase?" I ask, unable to hide the surprise in my voice.

He's unrepentant.

"I like you, Anna," he spurts out.

"You like me?"

*This is wrong. This is so totally wrong.*

"Yeah. Fuck," he's muttering. "I like you, Anna. There, I've said it."

"Chase, you shouldn't have kissed me."

"Why not?" he asks.

He knows why not. He *should* know.

"I'm not a cheater." I'm firm.

"But I like you, Anna."

I back away.

"How many times are you going to repeat that you like me, as if that's going to change my mind?"

He's firm as well. "As long as it takes."

"I'm not going to cheat on my fiancé, Chase. That was our terms from the start, alright? You know that. We shook on it."

"You can surely feel the connection between us, right?" he asks.

"Yeah, as *friends*."

"Not as anything more?"

"I am getting married. You know that."

"Yeah, but married to an asshole.," Chase says, and my mouth hangs open.

"Don't call Angus that."

Chase shrugs. "He is, though. You've practically said it yourself."

"No, I haven't," I reply, throwing my arms up. "All of this, all of this dancing and lessons and stripping were for *him.* Would I really think he's an asshole and go to all this effort to rekindle my relationship with him?"

Chase shakes his head at me. "Great, so you've gone to all this effort for him, but where is he tonight?"

"Um..."

*I have to admit, he's got me there.*

But it doesn't change the fact that I'm planning on getting married to the man, that I have made a commitment.

Chase certainly feels smug about saying something right that he continues. "Don't deny your feelings for me, Anna."

"*My* feelings?" I have to laugh at how insane this all is. I can't believe it's happening. "This is wrong, Chase. How many times do I have to say that I'm getting married?"

"So?"

"*So?* You can't be doing this."

"I met your fiancé, remember?" Chase asks, approaching me. I back further towards the door. "I met the guy, and it's clear as day he's not right for you."

"Right for me? How dare you assume what's right for me or not. You don't know me at all."

"I do know you," Chase replies slowly. "I know you so well, Anna. Does Angus bring you happiness? Freedom?"

"Happiness and freedom don't mean anything. They're just concepts. I'm looking for stability."

I'm regurgitating Dad's lines. It's like I'm a puppet and he's talking through me.

"Then what about love? Do you love him?" Chase asks me.

"What is wrong with you, Chase? Why are you like this?"

"He doesn't bring you any of these things, but I can. I know I can. You should be with me. I can't promise much in terms of money, but at least it's freedom."

I am flabbergasted by what this man's saying.

"Maybe I've been giving you the wrong signals, Chase. We're just friends."

"I don't think it's that at all. I think there's more than that. You know what's between us, you can't deny it."

He comes closer towards me. I push up against the door.

"This is wrong," I say under my breath. "So very wrong."

Chase stands still. He's so close to me.

He sighs.

"You have two choices, Anna. Him or me. You choose."

*No.*

"You can't make me choose between you or my fiancé, Chase."

"It's up to you."

*I can't.*

"Don't make me do this, Chase."

*Not this. Not now.*

"It's up to you."

And then I'm running out of there, out of the dressing room. Tears streaming down my face.

I don't want to choose. I don't want to be put into that situation.

Chase doesn't follow me.

*Thank God.*

I leave the club, wishing to never see the man again.

But, at the same time, I never want to lose him.

# 26

*CHASE*

Fuck.

Fuck.

Fuck.

*Well.*

I look stupid, don't I?

It's pretty safe to say *that* didn't go to plan.

I stand in my dressing room staring at the empty doorframe. Anna's just burst out of there in tears.

And I look like a complete idiot.

*Why did I do that? Why did I push her to make such an extreme decision?*

The kiss was so spontaneous. Look, I didn't even know I was going to kiss her until my lips were already on hers and by then it was too late.

It was like everything had clicked together in that kiss. All these weeks had been building up to that one moment. I truly realized right then when our lips collided that I had always been wanting to kiss her since the day we met again.

And she rejected me.

I know why. She's engaged. This shouldn't have happened. I get how she is adamant about not being a cheater. I understand totally.

But the kiss felt so right. We felt so right together.

Why couldn't she see that, too?

*Fuck.*

"What have you done?" I say out loud to myself.

*I'm such a fucking idiot.*

I don't know how to fix this. She's gone, and she may never come back.

I put her on the spot. I made her choose.

*And of course, she was going to choose her fiancé.*

I turn back to look at the present she gave me, at the painting of me on my bike. It's simply amazing. So thoughtful. She's put so much time and effort into it. No wonder it spurred me on to kiss her.

I'm so stupid. Why would I ever think a girl like her would want to go out with a guy like me?

I've been nothing but an utter idiot.

And I've now lost the one thing - the one *person* - who means anything and everything to me.

*Well, there's only one thing for me to do.*

* * *

I SLAM open my trailer door and immediately start pulling together everything I own. I grab my clothes and stuff them into my bag. I collect my last rolls of cash and fit them into my pockets.

I was right; I can pack up everything I own in just a matter of minutes.

My head is buzzing full of noise. Full of thoughts.

*Why did you kiss her? Why did you let yourself fall for her?*

I may be nothing but trailer trash, but at least I have my freedom. Anna, on the other hand, is going to be stuck in a loveless marriage for the rest of her life.

She can't say I didn't try to warn her.

She can't say I didn't offer her an escape.

But now she's chosen. And she chose not to be a cheater. I need to respect that, but that doesn't mean I have to stay living in this city.

I went too far.

I wish I could apologize, but I fear she never wants to see me again. That's fair.

I need to leave.

*BANG! BANG! BANG!*

Someone's knocking on my trailer door.

I roll my eyes.

I only can guess who this can be.

I open it.

Yep. It's Brandi.

She's got her hand pointed at me. "Where's the rest of the rent, Chase? You're so late. I've called my cousins and they're heading over right now." I brush past the woman, slinging my bag full of my possessions over my shoulder.

"You can call off your dogs, Brandi," I say. "I'm outta here right now. You're never going to see me again."

I fly onto my bike before she even has the chance to reply. I ignite my baby and zoom on out of there, leaving only a trail of dust behind.

I am correct, I am leaving. I am never going to see this city again.

My heart is too broken now.

And I know I am never going to see Anna again.

## 27

*ANNA*

IT WAS stupid of me to paint a picture of him. I shouldn't have done it on that canvas he gave me. It was definitely too much.

I wipe the tears from my eyes, trying hard to just focus on the road. I need to just get home and clear my head of Chase and that kiss.

*And that's going to be hard.*

I spin the steering wheel into the underground parking lot underneath Angus' apartment building.

I was stupid to think I could just paint a picture of the man and not give off the vibe that I wanted to be more than friends. But that honestly was not what I had intended at all.

Yeah, he's sexy. Yeah, we have great chemistry. Yeah, we've bonded so well in the last few weeks and he treats me good.

But I'm *engaged*.

That word means everything.

How many times do I need to repeat myself? I am *not* a cheater.

It was my fault for letting myself get too close to Chase. I should've seen this coming. I should've known he would make a move like he did in that dressing room. It was inevitable. We were like asteroids falling towards each other on an unstoppable collision course. I should've known how close we were getting.

A kiss was inevitable.

But it's ending now. I've done the right thing. I've ended it, and now I'm never going to see him again.

I ride the elevator up to my fiancé's apartment.

I'm going to tell Angus everything that's happened. Lay it all out on the table. Show him how much I love him and how much he should trust me.

I'm going to tell him the truth. Because that's what responsible adults do.

I'm going to tell him that I'm going to spend the rest of my life with him, that I am willing to make our marriage work, no matter our bumpy start. I'm in this for the long haul.

Because that's what a marriage is. Built upon trust.

I will make him love me again. We will touch each other again, even if that will take time. I'm willing to put in the effort.

I unlock the front door of Angus's apartment and step inside.

I feel strong now that I've made my choice. This is the right path.

The apartment feels empty when I walk in, but I know my fiancé must be home. He said he was going to stay in tonight rather than see my show.

"Angus?" I call out.

There's no answer.

But the lights are on. He always turns off the lights when he leaves. He must be here.

It's not even that late, but maybe he's already sleeping. I *am* home earlier than when I told him I would be. Maybe he didn't stay up to see me come in. I put my sports bag on the ground next to the kitchen counter and head over to the bedroom quietly, to not disturb him if he is in bed.

Maybe I'll have to talk to him tomorrow.

I slowly push open the bedroom door, expecting to find his shape curled up in bed.

He is there.

But he's not asleep.

The bed covers are moving. There's more than one shape. There's someone else in there.

Two people.

I take another step in.

And then I spot who it is in the bed.

Angus.

And Erin.

# 28

*ANNA*

"ERIN?"

I can't believe it. I just can't.

But she's there. In front of me. Lying in my bed. Clear as day.

My best friend. With my fiancé naked on top of her.

It only takes me a brief moment to understand what's happening. It takes only a brief moment for my whole world to fall apart.

They both stop when I speak.

They turn to me.

Angus looks unrepentant, almost annoyed, at me. As if me stumbling in to find him fucking my best friend is an annoyance that he'll have to tell me off for.

My hand drops from the door handle.

*Fuck.*

Erin stares at me in shock.

*No way this can be real.*

"I thought you wouldn't be back for another hour or two," Angus says, his voice flat.

"I can't believe this." My voice can't rise to beyond a whisper.

Everything is hazy.

"Anna, I am so sorry."

That's Erin.

*She's actually daring to speak right now?*

My best friend is actually trying to apologize? For this?

"I don't even want to hear your voice, Erin." I'm starting to shake. "Get out."

She's smart enough to know when to leave, and that time is right now.

I'm holding myself in from collapsing onto the floor. It is taking every ounce of me not to burst into tears.

But I've got to see this through. If my world is going to collapse, then I need to watch it happen.

Erin darts past me, completely naked, but I manage to grab her wrist before she has the chance to duck out the door.

"How long?" I ask, my voice trembling. "How long has this been going on for?"

My best friend is silent. She doesn't even look me in the eye. She drops her head.

*That's all I need from her.*

I can't bear to look at her anymore.

"You were my best friend," I say to her softly. "My *best* friend."

She doesn't reply.

I let her go, and she scurries away out of the room.

My heart is thumping out of my chest.

I turn back to my fiancé.

"How long?" I ask the naked man.

"It's just been tonight."

*Does he think I'm that stupid?*

"Don't bullshit me," I reply. "How long have you been screwing my best friend?"

Angus lets out a long sigh.

He must also know the engagement's over now.

"We're already done," I continue. "There's no reason to lie now. How long have you two been fucking for?"

"Months," he eventually replies.

I stagger against the bedroom wall, overcome with this realization.

Months.

No wonder he's paid me no attention for weeks. No wonder it's been like his heart's not in it anymore.

He really hasn't been from the very start.

*He's never loved me. All this time.*

"You've used me," I whisper. "You used me for your career. To get close to my dad. I'm nothing but a tool for you, aren't I?"

Angus says nothing. He just stares at me.

My head scrambles around, piecing the last few months together like a jigsaw. All my memories slot into place. I finally understand everything, all those times Angus would never touch me. All the times he seemed disinterested.

*This* was the reason why.

So that means...

"Those dance lessons Erin paid for me. They were just an excuse to get me out of the apartment for the both of you to do... this?"

Angus still doesn't say anything. He doesn't need to. His silence tells me everything I need to know.

I fall back on the wall. I can barely stand. My legs have turned to jelly.

I look at him. I look at my naked fiancé sitting there

awkwardly on the end of our bed like a worm, and I just feel a profound sense of betrayal.

And loss.

Yep. My whole world really has fallen apart.

"Well, you two are good together. I hope you find your happiness," I say.

They are the last words I ever say to Angus before I leave his life forever.

I walk out that door and never look back.

# 29

*ANNA*

I STOP the car outside the trailer park and slam my fist against the steering wheel.

And then I take in a long breath.

It doesn't calm me down.

I don't know why I've come here. I don't know why I've driven all the way across the city. It was completely unplanned.

I needed somewhere to go after I stormed out of Angus's place, and when I got in the car, I just instinctively drove to this goddamn trailer park. There's no one else to turn to. Where else do you go when both your best friend and your fiancé betray you in the worst of ways?

Images flash before my eyes again. Erin and Angus in my bed. Their naked bodies pushed against each other.

*I don't even know who I am anymore.*

First Chase, and now Erin and Angus. I've lost everyone in one night.

I put my foot down and drive through the gates, right up

through the trailer park, until I reach Chase's trailer on the far side.

I need to see him. Right now. I need to talk to someone who understands. Not my mother, and certainly not my father. I've lost my best friend and my fiancé and I don't know where to go or what to do.

I only trust Chase. He's the only person on planet earth who understands me. The only person who can comfort me right now.

It's late. The lights are not on inside his place. There's no motorcycle outside.

But the door is open.

*That's strange.*

Cautiously, I open the car door and step up to the open trailer. I peek inside.

There's a woman moving about in there. I've never seen her before.

And she's definitely not the type of woman Chase would be sleeping with.

So why is she here?

"Hello?" I ask, knocking on the side of the trailer to get her attention.

It works. The woman turns. She glares at me.

"Who are you?" she asks sternly.

"I'm Anna, Chase's friend. I'm looking for him."

"He's not here." She's curt.

"Do you know where he's gone?" I ask.

The woman shrugs. She sneers at me aggressively. I think I better leave before she rips my head off.

"He says he's gone. If you do see him, tell him he owes me rent," she says. "Unless you want to pay it? You're a friend of his?"

She makes a quick move towards me.

*Okay, definitely time to go.*

I stumble away from her and rush back to the car. I quickly turn on the ignition.

I spin out of the trailer park, away from this crazy woman.

I need to see him. But she says he's gone.

And then I remember what he said to me that one time in his trailer, how he said that he's prepared to just leave at any moment. How he's free to travel whenever and wherever he likes.

That means he might already be gone. That means I might never see him again.

I am filled with dread.

*Have I lost him forever?*

As I drive back to the city, I try his phone. I know he hates using it, but right now, it's my only lifeline back to him. I pray to God he hasn't destroyed the SIM card or anything. That would be a very Chase thing to do.

I just need to see him.

I need to hear his voice.

The call rings. My heart stops.

*Come on, please.*

I beg silently at my phone. At his name flashing on my screen.

But he doesn't pick up.

## 30

*CHASE*

"This is it, Toby," I say to Xstasy's manager.

"This is what?"

"Goodbye, I guess."

He looks at me, startled, from across his desk. I don't blame him. I would be startled too if my best money-making act had just rocked up in my office and abruptly said farewell.

I can practically see the metaphorical dollars burning up in his eyes as I speak.

"What?" he asks. "You're leaving?"

"Yep."

"For good?"

I raise my hand. "There's no point trying to stop me."

It doesn't take him a beat to start coming up with his usual hustler schtick.

"Is it your pay? We can negotiate it if it's a sticky point. I'm prepared to negotiate a lot of things, Chase, to keep you here."

I shake my head. "Nope. It's not about the pay at all. Personal stuff."

"Right, I see," Toby replies. He's a smart enough guy to realize there's no chance I'll stay, and he's also smart enough to know not to ask why. "Where are you gonna go?"

I shrug. "Dunno. Maybe Las Vegas. Los Angeles. Somewhere west. As long as I'm out of this city."

"That bad?" I don't respond. Toby offers his hand, a rare act of humanity from him. "I'm sorry to see you go."

I lean across his desk and shake his hand. "Me too."

"You were one hell of an act. Damn, now I'll have to rely on Ryan's Tarzan shit."

"I HEARD that you are leaving. One final drink for the road, then?"

I glance up at the bartender. "You know me too well, Stacy."

She gives me a cheeky smile before sliding a beer bottle down the counter. I nod at her before tasting the cold liquid.

*Yep, one final drink for the road.*

"What a shame. I'll miss you," Stacy says. "You always added some spice to this place. I swear to God, if I see Ryan's Tarzan thing again, I'm going to go crazy."

"Ah, Ryan. Why else do you think I'm leaving?"

She laughs and strolls down to the other side of the bar.

"I saw you dancing the other night."

Someone's joined me. She sits on the stool next to mine. A young blonde girl. Around twenty.

*What is it with this bar and chicks hitting on me?*

"You did?" I ask her.

She looks like a model. A real looker. Someone who I bet would be lots of fun in the bedroom.

I take another sip of the beer. The girl stares at me, watching me with hunger in her eyes.

Yep, I know that look.

"Maybe you could show me some of those moves in private," she says, her hand resting on my thigh.

She's fast, I give her that. She knows what she wants.

"Somewhere private, huh?"

She leans forward, whispering in my ear. Her chest presses into my arm. She's pushing her breasts right up against me. "I'm from out of town, and I'm staying in a motel around the corner. Maybe you can show me your moves there."

*Wow. She's really hungry for it.*

I slowly shake my head. "Not today..."

"Elena," she says, finishing my sentence.

I point to my chest. "Chase," I reply. "Not today, Elena."

She blinks at me. "Why not?"

"Just not today."

She stares at me for a long while. I stare back. Her eyes seem to penetrate my soul.

"There's a girl, isn't there?" she eventually asks, as if coming to an almost-spiritual revelation.

*Damn, for being so fast, she's also very perceptive.*

I'm lost for words. I don't reply.

"I can tell," she continues. "I can tell when someone's in love, and you definitely are. I see it in your eyes. Your mind is on someone right now."

"You're good, Elena," I reply quietly. "Real good."

"So, it's true?"

I ignore that question. "How do you know how to do that?" I ask instead.

She shrugs. "I can just tell these things."

"Well, you should probably start charging people for it. Start a stall at a fair."

"Maybe I should. How about I get you a drink and we can talk about this mysterious girl?" she asks, nodding at the bar.

"You're good, Elena, but not that good," I say, rising from my seat and away from her thrusting breasts. "I would love to stay, but I have to go."

She's disappointed, but I don't care. "Sure."

I wink at Stacy down the bar. She blows me a kiss in return. We're both pros on the stripper circuit. We don't need to have an emotional goodbye.

*Time to get out of Xstasy. Forever.*

I head out the exit into the parking lot of the club. All my stuff is with my bike. I can leave the city right now without ever needing to look back. Exactly what I want.

It's time to hit the open road again.

I'll find another place. Another city. Another strip club to perform in. I'll do what I always do.

But this time will be different.

This time I'll be doing this with my heart broken.

*One girl has really got you cut up, right Chase?*

Yep. And it somehow hurts more than any physical fight I've ever been in.

Outside the club, the night air is cool. Above me, the city skyline is lit up into the stars. I can see Jensen tower rising up in the middle of downtown. It's hard to avoid it when it's the biggest building in the city.

*Well, I can avoid it when I'm out of here on the highway in a few minutes. I'll never have to think about Anna Jensen again.*

I turn the corner where I've parked my motorcycle.

A person is sitting on my bike.

*Oh shit. What the fuck?*

My hands curl into fists, ready for a fight.

But then I see it's Anna.

She's sitting on my bike, smiling at me.

"What are you doing?" I ask her, breathless.

Anna doesn't seem surprised to see me. She's clearly been waiting for me to emerge from Xstasy. She's been sitting out here on my bike as if she's my girl.

*But she's not my girl.*

"You were right," she replies, her hands gripping my bike's handlebars. "I do have two choices. You or Angus. And I choose you."

"You do?"

She nods. "I do."

That's all I need to know.

But I see her face. I'm not an idiot; I can see she's been crying. Something's happened, but whatever it is, she can tell me in her own time.

What's important right now is that she chooses me.

And I know exactly where to take her. I'm not going to waste this moment.

"Anna, for what I did back there tonight..."

She raises a hand, stopping me before I can properly apologize for that kiss.

"You don't need to say anything. Sure, it was wrong. But you were also right. A lot has happened since then."

I know it's my turn to stop. To not press her.

She's here now. That's the critical thing.

The woman I thought I'd never see again is right in front of me. I'm not going to lose her again.

"Come with me," I reply as I slide onto the motorcycle in front of her. She wraps her arms around me and rests her head on my back.

And then I start up my bike.

# 31

*ANNA*

I ʜᴜɢ Chase around his waist as we zoom down the city's streets, going some place I do not know. We are definitely heading downtown, that much I can tell. But where? I can't guess.

It's only when we pull up in front of the familiar building that I realize where he's taken me, and then I laugh hysterically.

"Really, Chase?" I ask as he parks the bike. "The dance studio?"

He turns his head and smiles at me. "Yep."

I look around at the empty streets and the dim street-lights. "It's the middle of the night, Chase. It isn't even open, you crazy man."

He helps me off his motorcycle before pulling out something from his leather jacket pocket. I can see it's a set of keys that he spins around on his finger. They glint in the darkness.

"I've made a copy," he says smugly.

"Keys? For this place?" My mouth hangs open. I honestly don't know how he's managed to pull this off. "How on earth did you manage that?"

He gives me a wink. The smug bastard. "Oh, I have my ways, Anna. Trust me."

"How though?"

"I know a lot of bad shit. When you're a broke stripper you just have to."

"Tell me."

"You don't want to know."

"You sneaking around like that, stealing keys. Being a criminal. It's kinda hot," I reply. I make a move towards him. My hands start to reach for his perfect face.

"I *am* a bad boy," he declares.

*Well, that ruins the mood.*

And he knows exactly what he's doing with his silly humor. Winding me up. As always.

I roll my eyes. "Shut it. I shouldn't have said anything."

"You love it."

He flashes another smile at me before bounding up to the front door. I grab his hand before he can unlock it.

"Isn't this going to be, like, totally illegal?" I ask nervously.

"Depends on how you view it."

He's such a goddamn rebel. I can tell he's loving provoking me up like this. Freaking me out. The bad boy stripper scaring the rich uptight girl by *actually* breaking in somewhere.

It *is* kinda hot, but I can't shut my brain off from thinking that this is going to be a terrible idea.

"Maybe view it from a judge's perspective?" I suggest. "You know, from the inside of a courtroom?"

"I've never done that before," he replies. "Why start now?"

"I really don't want to be caught breaking into a dance studio, of all places."

He chuckles. "Live a little, Anna."

*Ugh.*

He's so infuriating.

Chase unlocks the door, and we step into the dark and empty dance studio.

He quickly presses a code into the alarm system to disable it. I shake my head at him.

I really don't want to know how he learned that code.

He takes my hand in his and leads me upstairs to our regular rehearsal room.

It's even darker in there. Pitch-black. I can't see a single thing when we get inside.

Chase lets go of my hand and for a brief moment, I'm in a panic.

I'm lost in the dark.

"Chase?" I call out. "Chase?"

"Right here."

Suddenly, lights turn on inside our studio. Dim lights. And as soon as the lights turn on, the music starts. A loud thudding beat fills the room with noise.

Chase is behind me. He takes my shoulders and pulls me down into a chair. I'm so bewildered by the sudden lights and sounds that I just let him do so.

And then he's in front of me.

And he's dancing to the beat. His body shakes. His hips thrust. His hands travel across his sweaty body.

He's stripping.

Just for me.

He moves closer towards me. I'm smiling at him, smiling at the serious pout he's giving me.

It's super sexy.

And then he leans over me.

Our lips are close. I can feel his warm breath on my face. My heart is beating uncontrollably.

*This is what I want.*

I want to taste his mouth again.

And then he sits in my lap. I feel the weight of him on top of me as he worms his way out of his shirt, revealing his ripped torso. All his hard muscles. His killer abs. His hands slide up to my face, and he begins to thrust, dry-humping me. I giggle.

It's not every day you get a private dance from a male stripper.

Especially not from one you know really wants to *fuck* you.

I finger his rock-solid pecs, squealing even more as his body rocks into mine.

He leans closer, still not smiling. Pouting.

"You're taking this so seriously," I say, breathless.

"Shut up," he whispers back before he kisses me.

And I fall into his kiss guilt-free.

This is what I've truly desired for the last seven weeks. My engagement with Angus was never real, even before I found out about him and Erin. I should've seen it was always Chase my heart was longing for, not the man Dad had set up for me.

This was where I was always meant to be. In Chase's arms.

As he kisses me, I unbuckle his belt. Then I pull down his jeans far enough that I can take his cock in my hands. I start to stroke, watching with glee as he moans and shakes to my touch. I love what I'm able to do to him.

With a grunt, he pulls away from me. His hands pull my top over my head.

"I'm still sweaty from the dance earlier," I say. I can't believe it was only a few hours ago we were both on stage at

Xstasy grinding in front of a live audience. That was before my world fell apart because of Angus and then was put together by Chase.

"Me too," he replies before he slides out of his jeans so that he is fully naked in front of me. "I like it when you're sweaty."

I involuntarily giggle at the sight of his toned body.

For the first time since we've stepped foot into the dance studio, Chase cracks a smile.

"What you laughing at?" he asks.

"You're just too handsome."

His smile somehow gets wider.

"Well, let me see you, then."

"No way. Not after the way you look."

He ignores me and rips off my jeans so that I'm also naked.

The look he gives me... it's so full of *lust*. Passion. I'm so turned on by how much he's turned on.

He dives down to my pussy like he's thirsting for it.

*No problem with me,*

"I've missed this," he says. I know exactly what he's talking about. I've missed that night six months ago, and he clearly does, too. "Let me taste you."

My back arches as his tongue finds its way across my wet sex. I gasp as he plays with my clit between his lips.

He knows how to play me, how to tease me. How to bring out those waves of pleasure that crash within my soul.

I'm gagging for him.

As he brings me to climax, he stops. Right at the cliff's edge.

"What are you doing?" I ask, completely out of breath.

*I need him so badly.*

He leans up so that his lips gently brush my ear. "I'm

going to make you feel things you've never felt before, Anna."

"Yes, please," I whisper back.

He fishes in his jeans pocket for a condom.

I close my eyes, my body shivering with anticipation for what's about to happen next.

I still keep my eyes closed as his warm hands wrap around my hips. I feel his body slide into place between my open legs. I can feel something long and thick between his own legs.

*It's coming.*

And then he enters me.

His body entwines with mine. He pushes up deep inside me. And then he moves to the music enveloping the room like a true dancer. He's strong and yet so gentle. A bad boy with a soft heart just for me.

He's more passionate than Angus ever was. Chase's desire for me is so overpowering. So intense. He wants my body. He wants me deep in his soul.

And I want him in mine.

A soft moan escapes from between my wet lips as he thrusts. His hand reaches around and cups my ass. Squeezing.

He was right. He is making me feel things I have never felt before.

He comes to climax, moaning and softly kissing my open lips as he shakes.

"I want you to cum, Chase," I whisper. "I want you so bad."

As if on my command, he groans loudly.

And then he says my name over and over as he cums.

"Anna, Anna, *Anna.*"

And I say his over and over.

"Chase. Captain Chase."

# 32

*ANNA*

"Angus cheated on me."

I stop what I'm doing and turn to Anna. She's fully clothed now. I can't make her out properly in the dim lighting of the dance studio, but I think I can see tears streaming from her eyes. Her cheeks glisten with the droplets.

She's crying.

"Is that what happened?" I ask.

She slowly nods.

"He... it was with Erin."

My body freezes. I'm still getting changed. My pants are on but I'm topless.

Did I hear that right? Her fiancé was cheating on her with her best friend?

*Fuck.*

That's rough.

"I caught them in the act," she murmurs. I can hear the

wavering emotion in her voice and my heart reaches out for her.

"I'm sorry."

I gently wrap my arms around her shaking body, embracing her close. She doesn't put up any resistance.

"They were there, in my bed, when I got home tonight."

"I'm sorry."

She presses her face against my bare shoulder. Her hands tightly hug around me.

I know she needs me right now.

*And I'm here for her.*

"I walked in and they were there."

"Is that why you came to find me?" I ask.

She takes in a deep breath.

"I didn't know what to do or who to turn to."

"I see," I reply. "And you didn't know?"

"About Erin or Angus?" She can barely even say their names. "No. I didn't even suspect a thing."

My hand brushes through her hair. She smells of sweat and me. "I am so sorry."

We stand still, hugging, for a long time. I keep on gently rubbing my fingers through her hair as she cries softly into my chest.

"You know the worst thing is?" she asks between sobs. "The craziest thing about it all?"

"What?"

"They've been using these dance lessons as a way to make sure I'm out of the picture every week, as a way to go behind my back."

"Wow."

"He made me feel like I was in the wrong so much for trying to improve our relationship. He made me feel wrong for trying to be appealing to him. For going to these lessons to feel sexy again. He really made me feel shit about doing so. But, at the same time, he was fucking my best friend. All that time, that was what he was doing. Behind my back. I never knew. I never guessed at any moment that they were together. He accused me of cheating with you whilst he was screwing my best friend."

"I'm so sorry, Anna."

"I should've guessed. I should've sussed out what was going on between them."

"You couldn't have."

"Am I really that stupid?"

"You're not stupid, Anna."

"Am I too stupid to not tell when my best friend and fiancé are fucking?"

"You're not stupid. They deceived you."

"I just don't know anymore."

"Listen to me," I say, bending down and bringing her face level with mine. "You did nothing wrong, Anna. Nothing at all. It was all Angus and Erin. They fucked up. They lost a friend and a fiancée because of their selfish, stupid actions. You are not to blame, alright?"

"Okay."

I can tell she's still unsure. Still hesitant.

"You came here to learn how to be sexy for your fiancé. You took lessons from me because you wanted to spark up your relationship, and you never, ever wanted to cheat on him. You've done nothing wrong. He's an incredibly stupid man if he doesn't realize what he's lost. You are the most beautiful, smart, talented woman I've ever met, Anna."

"Yeah?"

"I love you."

"What?"

I say it again. Louder. So she can hear what I'm really saying. "I *love* you, Anna Jensen."

She looks up at me.

And then she kisses me.

Angus may not realize what he's lost, but I know what I've gained. The *world*.

Anna means everything to me. That's what I've come to realize these last seven weeks.

She's my soulmate.

I can't live without her.

I thought I would never have a woman. I thought no female would ever tie me down.

But then I met Anna. And then I fell in love.

We pause. Our heads press together, her cute nose burrowing into my cheek.

This is where I want to be for the rest of my life, forget about the clubs, or the money, or the girls. This is where I should be. My body next to Anna's.

I laugh. "I guess I probably won't be getting the rest of the dance money, then?"

And then Anna laughs too.

# 33

ONE WEEK LATER

*ANNA*

I sQUEEZE my arms even tighter around Chase as we speed down the empty highway. His leather jacket is warm, and I can feel the outline of his muscles underneath as I hold on for dear life.

But I've never felt happier.

I look up at Chase. His face is fixated on the road ahead. His sunglasses reflect the light as we speed past nothing but a barren wasteland. We're on the back of his motorcycle, driving in a random direction. We have no plan. No destination. There are no other vehicles about. The sun is just starting to set beyond the horizon and the sky is filled with red.

I feel like I'm in the opening line of that *Hotel California* song.

It's been a crazy week to lead us to where we are now on

the back of this roaring bike. A week full of tears and pain, but also a week full of joy and happiness.

I sold all my stuff. A *very* Chase move, I know, but it was actually completely my decision. I wanted to get rid of all these unnecessary things that were doing nothing but anchoring myself into a life I didn't want.

I sold everything except the things that were precious to me. Everything that didn't mean something to me. Anything that wasn't useful for a life on the road. And I found that there were a lot fewer things saved than I expected.

*A new life. A new start.*

Then I quit my job. Dad wasn't too happy about that, but after what happened with Angus, he didn't have much power over me anymore. I didn't even go into the office again. I just called him up one day and told him that I would no longer be working as his receptionist. He already knew about my fiancé's actions. Everybody knew when the word got out. Gossip spreads pretty fast in the ultra-rich circles, and this was some *extra* juicy gossip.

And my father couldn't do shit to persuade me to stay.

"And what are you going to do with your life now?" Dad had asked me on the line after I resigned. He intended it as a taunt, but I decided to answer it, anyway.

"I honestly don't know, Dad. Maybe find some happiness."

And then I hung up.

And the truth is, I honestly don't know what I'm going to do with my life. But one thing is for sure, sitting on the back of Chase's motorcycle, I finally start to feel it for the first time. I finally start to feel this thing I've only heard others talk about so much.

Happiness.

# EPILOGUE

## TWO YEARS LATER

I sit down on the bar stool with a grunt.

"Sparkling water?"

I glance over at the bartender behind the bar with a smile on my lips.

"You know me so well, Stacy," I say.

She gives me a wink and hands me an opened bottle of cold water. I take it with a thanks.

"He should be any minute now," Stacy says, nodding at the stage.

"Let's hope he doesn't try that Tarzan routine that crashed and burned last week," I reply, and the bartender laughs.

I relax into the stool and turn to face the rest of the club. The place is crammed with customers tonight and it's only Tuesday. It should be one of our quietest days. But tonight, we are full.

*We know how to put on a show.*

I glance around the room, past the squealing drunk

women waiting impatiently for the performance, and to the walls of the club. We've decorated the place with my own artwork.

My eyes linger on one particular painting of mine. Chase on his motorcycle, looking all suave and cocky. The one I'd given to him two years ago at Xstasy after our dance together, on the same canvas he had given me.

My heart warms every time I see that painting, and now is no different. That was the first of many paintings, so many that now I'm a fully qualified art teacher with my own class every weekend. It's a job made from my dreams.

I still get my head over the fact that I'm an art teacher, even when I have a full class of students in front of me.

There's a short pain from my belly, a little baby kick. I'm heavily pregnant.

The whole thing was kind of an accident, but a *very* happy accident. Chase and I never even thought about kids properly, and then this happened. But immediately once we found out there was one on the way, we realized it's the best thing that could ever happen to us.

And the little guy in there likes to move around. A lot. It's like he's dancing.

*I wonder who he's inherited that from?*

Chase has gone absolutely *goo-goo* over the baby. He's repainted a room in the house. Bought a bunch of baby stuff. I think he really wants to be super involved in this kid's life. It's like his whole personality has changed and he's transformed into full-on daddy mode. And I know he's going to be a great dad.

One thing's for sure though, our baby is *not* going to have a stripper name.

The club lights dim. The show's about to start. The crowd goes ecstatic.

I plug my fingers in my ears to block out the noise. Even

though I co-own this club in Los Angeles with Chase, I still can't get used to the wall of squealing that alcohol-induced women produce when they've been promised a half-naked muscle man.

We bought this club just over a year ago. We didn't know what the hell we were doing, but we still jumped in, nonetheless. And, through hard work and many sleepless nights, we made it a success. We're one of the most popular male strip clubs in the city. We brought Stacy along when we opened. She was happy to get the hell out of Xstasy.

We opened to full houses every night, and the rest, as they say, is history.

And you know what?

I'm finally *happy*.

Chase told me his stripper rules, especially the one about *not* fucking your co-workers. I told him that technically I am his co-working, seeing that we both own this club, so *technically* he did break one of his unbreakable rules.

Chase didn't mind. He's always been a rule breaker.

And let's just say, I don't mind it either.

So much for *Little Miss Stuck-Up*.

The announcer comes on stage. He's holding a microphone in his hands.

Stacy winks at me.

We both know what's coming.

"Are you lovely ladies ready for the main event?"

*Yes!*

"The one you sexy women are all here tonight for?"

*Yes!*

"The one that knows exactly what to do to get you all hot and bothered?"

*Yes!*

"He's going to give you his marching orders. Wait until you see his weapon."

*Yes!*

"If you want him, he's locked and loaded."

*YES!*

"You know who he is. Give it up for the one and only... *CAPTAIN CHASE.*"

The curtain falls away.

Chase stands there, posing. His muscles bulging. His pout strong.

Looking every inch the sexy hunk he is.

The music gets louder. The screaming intensifies.

And my husband, like the pro he is, starts to strip.

# ABOUT THE AUTHOR

Rebecca has had the storytelling bug since... forever!

What Rebecca likes most is writing steamy hot filthy romances with sweet happy endings sprinkled with some delicious bad boys.

Born and raised in an Aussie coastal town, she loves travelling around the world - meeting new people and discovering their stories.

Aside from adventuring she also enjoys a good rainy day in with a good book or at a hot beach catching the sun.

She's a world-class napping professional. You'll most likely find her asleep snuggled up on a sofa somewhere cozy.

For other titles and information please visit
rebeccacastle.com

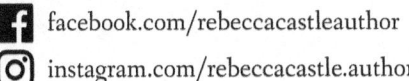 facebook.com/rebeccacastleauthor
instagram.com/rebeccacastle.author